*Other books by*
NATALIE SAVAGE CARLSON

The Happy Orpheline
*Pictures by Garth Williams*

A Brother for the Orphelines
*Pictures by Garth Williams*

The Family Under the Bridge
*Pictures by Garth Williams*

Sashes Red and Blue
*Pictures by Rita Fava*

Wings Against the Wind
*Pictures by Mircea Vasiliu*

The Talking Cat
and other stories of french canada
*Pictures by Roger Duvoisin*

# The

# Tomahawk Family

by Natalie Savage Carlson

*Pictures by Stephen Cook*

*JC 198 to*

HARPER & BROTHERS

*Publishers* NEW YORK

For
LESLEY BROKENLEG,
*the son of our friend, Noah Brokenleg*

# The

# Tomahawk Family

# I

IN THE MOON when the leaves of schoolbooks begin to turn, two Indian children were spending the last days of their summer vacation thinking about the new school year. They lived with their grandmother on a Sioux reservation in South Dakota. They lived in a log cabin with corners like clasped fingers—as if they were holding the family tightly together. But logs were not strong enough to hold the Tomahawks together because they were a divided family.

Alice Tomahawk was happy that they would soon be taking the bus every day for the Little Axe school on the reservation. She was eight years old, and she wanted to learn as much as she could so that she would be a good American.

But her older brother, Frankie, wasn't sure. It was not being sure about many things which made everything so hard. Sometimes he thought that he wanted to be a good American and become a tribal policeman or own a big ranch when he grew up. Most of the time he wished that he could be a brave warrior galloping across the plains like the old-time Indians he often saw on Abel White Eagle's TV screen.

It had been easier then for a Sioux boy to know what road to follow. He went into the wilderness alone and prayed and fasted until the vision came which showed him his way.

Frankie was a wiry boy of ten with a thin serious face and a scalplock of black hair. No matter how hard he brushed his hair, it always stood on end. The storekeeper said that it was because of the cowlicks on his head, but Frankie knew that he had never been licked by a cow.

Right now he and Alice weren't thinking about school. They were thinking about the big picnic at Oak Grove. It would be the last one of the summer and the announcement hanging in the store invited everyone on the reservation to attend the park celebration. Admission was fifty cents a car.

The White Eagle family was going to pick them up and take them to the celebration. "It only costs for the car," said Mrs. White Eagle, "so we will squeeze in as many as possible. But we can't stay all weekend like the others. We're driving back right after the afternoon dances. I have a lot of work to do to get the children ready for school."

But Frankie knew that Mr. and Mrs. White Eagle were returning early so they wouldn't miss their favorite TV show. Abel was lucky. He was riding his horse to Oak Grove so that he could stay at the celebration as long as he wished.

"Won't you go?" Alice asked Grandma. "You were invited and it won't cost you anything."

Grandma Tomahawk was squatting in the shade of the squaw cooler, playing her favorite game.

The cooler stood beside the Tomahawk cabin. It was a shelter made of forked poles thrust into the ground and covered with leafy branches cut from trees. It served the Indians in the same way that terraces and patios serve white people.

Grandma's puckered and weather-beaten face looked like a pine cone. Her thin braids were whitened by the snows of many winters, but her eyes looked as strong and sharp as a hawk's. At Alice's words, she screwed her lips tightly together although there were no front teeth to hold them in place.

"No," said Grandma tightly. "They don't want me on council. Me not go to their powwow."

It had been an insult to Grandma that she hadn't been elected to the tribal council. Two younger women sat on it and they weren't even the daughters of chiefs as she was.

She went back to playing her game of "five centses." Grandma had made up the game herself. During the summer she spent much of her time loitering in front of the store near the Agency. If tourists tried to take her picture, she would hold out her hand and demand, "Five cents."

She would look at the proffered nickel carefully. If it had a buffalo on one side and a Sioux on the other, she would pose for the picture. But if it was the Great White Father and his tepee, she would return the coin and cover her face with her shawl.

Some of the coins were laid out with the Indian heads up and the others buffalo up. Then she took turns rolling an Indian at the buffaloes to see how many he could hit. These were turned into Indians. When all the buffaloes were gone, the game was ended.

Grandma cackled with glee and rocked back and forth on the heels of her moccasins.

"Buffalo all gone," she cried triumphantly. "Me win game."

Frankie stared down at the pile of Indian heads.

"What are your Indians going to eat now?" he asked. "They will starve."

Grandma smiled mischievously then began turning the coins over. "Buffalo come back," she declared. "Just like Crazy Jim say. You want play game with me?" she asked Alice.

"No," said Alice, shaking her loose black hair. She had a plump face like a little copper moon and the quick movements of a chickaree. "It's a silly game," she said scornfully. "They didn't play it at school. Why don't you fix our house up nice, Grandma, instead of always sitting in the dirt and playing that silly game?"

"It is a good game," said Grandma in the Sioux tongue. "I always win."

Alice's cheeks flushed. "Why do you always act Indian, Grandma?" she asked reproachfully. "You went to a mission school when you were a little girl. Why don't you talk good English like me and Frankie?" she went on unhappily. "Why do you always loaf around and not make our house pretty? You learned good American stuff at the mission school."

"School burn down," replied Grandma, and she started a new game.

"You let Grandma alone." Frankie scowled. "She can be an Indian if she wants."

"I'm trying to help her," said Alice. "Teacher said we should help our parents become good citizens. She's the only parents we have now."

"You can't help people if they don't want to be helped," said Frankie, remembering how hard his teacher had tried to teach him the multiplication tables.

"I'm going to make her want to be helped," insisted Alice. "Teacher said—"

"Aw, teacher said, teacher said," echoed Frankie. "My teacher said, too, Little Big Ears, but I didn't listen."

"That's why you got bad marks last year," retorted Alice. "That's why you didn't pass and have to be in the fourth grade again with me."

Frankie put his hands over his ears and went to the tent pitched on the other side of the cabin.

Then Alice began feeling ashamed of the way she had talked to her grandmother. She squatted beside the old woman and spun a coin in the dust. She wanted to tell Grandma that she was sorry, but words didn't come easily to Alice when they had to come to her tongue all the way from her heart.

"But I love you, Grandma," she said shyly, "even if you aren't civilized. And I wish you would go to the picnic with us."

# II

THE WHITE EAGLE family came driving over for Frankie and Alice in the early afternoon. They knew the car was coming long before they could see it because Mr. White Eagle always announced his arrival by turning the switch on and off to make sounds like gunfire. He had learned that this brought people out faster than honking.

All the White Eagles except Abel were in the car. They shared it with Mrs. Tall Cow and her children and two dogs. More laps were made available and the dogs were pushed to the floor. Alice and Frankie were cheerfully squeezed in.

It had been a hot, dry summer. The fierce sun was still shooting his fiery arrows earthward. They had burned the grass and killed the small streams. Even the tall sunflowers looked as if they were tired of all the sunshine.

As Mr. White Eagle raced his car down the road, he left a cloud of dust behind him. They roared between lonely stretches of sunburned fields and past stunted cornfields. They passed ranch shacks with their outhouses, windmills and squaw coolers. Each ranch was a cluster of shelters and sometimes there were horses or cattle in the nearby corral. Nearly every house had a few rusted automobile bodies lying in the yard, as if the owner wanted to boast of how many cars he had owned.

Every time Mr. White Eagle passed a ranch, he would make his car fire like a gun so that the people inside would know that the White Eagles were on their way to the park celebration.

They shot and fired through a good-sized town of frame buildings, a store and post office combined and a white church with a tall steeple.

The park was in a ravine cooled by big oaks and a broad creek. Many of the Indians had already arrived and their trucks and automobiles were parked all around the entrance.

"Hurry! Hurry!" Gloria Jean cried to her father. But the White Eagle car had to crawl through a fog of dust into the park because there were so many people on foot in the road ahead. Finally Mr. White Eagle had to park behind a tent.

"Look at all those tents!" shouted Frankie.

They had sprung up in the grove like pasqueflowers on a springtime prairie. Men, women and children were going their separate ways around them like busy ants.

Frankie's throat tightened with excitement. This must have been the way it was in the old days when the Indians set up their tepees in a new camp.

Alice was excited too. She couldn't help enjoying it. Now she and Gloria Jean White Eagle would be seeing many school friends they had missed during the summer.

"Listen to the drums!" cried Frankie.

He jumped out of the car and hurried toward the rumbling sound. In a cleared part of the grove two proud American flags rose tall as the oak trees. Their poles were painted red, white and blue.

Frankie looked at the flags ruffled by the breeze. He knew that they were in memory of Sioux soldiers who had died fighting for the United

States in the great world wars. It made him proud to know that modern Indians had been brave warriors too.

Long planks had been set up on empty cans to make a circle of seats. There was a grandstand made like a great squaw cooler on one side. Old women with braids and fringed summer shawls sat on the planks, gossiping together in their gobbly native tongue.

"They're calling everybody to dinner," said Mrs. White Eagle. "Let's get in line."

Committee men wearing red badges presided over the huge black cauldrons of soup and beef. The picnickers had brought their own pans and cups. Into each pan was poured soup, and a big hunk of beef was splashed into the center. The coffee cups were filled.

"Here's some dessert." A committee man winked as he sneaked some lumps of sugar to Frankie and the other children.

They sat under the scissored leaves of the oaks, hungrily eating their rations. Frankie wished that Grandma had come because she loved beef so much and had so little of it at home.

The picnickers sucked the soup from the bowls and held the meat in their fingers. The children played as they ate and some of them spilled their soup or dropped their meat which was eagerly seized by the slinking dogs.

The beat of the drums and the chants of "hai-yai" made the very trees throb.

"You have finished eating," cried the announcer over the loud-speaker. "Now it is time to dance and shake your food down."

Many of the people had brought the colorful Indian clothing and ornaments which they had purchased at the handicraft store in town. They were made by skillful old Sioux who still knew how to tan hides, sew beads in intricate designs and dye eagle feathers.

Now those who wanted to dance would go to their tents and dress up. Frankie wished that he had some Indian clothes, but they were too expensive for the Tomahawk children. Grandma had a beautiful beaded costume made by her own grandmother, and she had worn it once to a pageant in the Black Hills.

"It's time to dance," cried the loud-speaker.

"Have you eaten so much that you can't move?"

The older women wriggled restlessly on the planks and raised their knees in time to the drumbeats. One of them stood up and began a shuffling step.

At last a tinkle of bells came down the hill from the tents. It was made by the men dressed in beaded garments with feathers in their hair and clusters of large bells around their ankles.

The drums rumbled like thunderbirds. The women stopped chattering. A crowd gathered behind the seated ones. Abel White Eagle rode his horse up behind Frankie, and the horse nuzzled Frankie's scalplock.

In the olden times, the braves had danced like this before a battle or a hunt. Frankie imagined the white tents to be painted tepees. He imagined that there were no roads or houses beyond the park— only wild prairie and the great herds of buffalo. He looked up into the sky. The spell was broken by the two waving flags. The painted tepees and the buffalo herds were gone forever and the sway-

ing warriors were reservation Indians at the annual park celebration.

It was then that Abel White Eagle called down to him. "You want to ride Spot?" he asked. "You can take a long ride because I'm going to get into my buckskins and dance with the men."

Frankie hated to leave the dancing but he knew that it was probably his only chance to have a ride on the spotted horse. He gave it a lump of sugar. Then Abel guided the horse sideways so that Frankie could mount it from the plank.

Frankie drove the horse away from the crowd. He headed it down the creek, out of the grove and into the prairie. Pink-breasted doves were dusting themselves in bare patches. A redtail hawk sitting on a fence post stared at Frankie with Grandma's eyes.

The boy looked ahead and remembered that over yonder where the line of creek cottonwoods and aspens curved between low hills lived his old friend, Jim Sees Hawk. It had been a month since the boy had seen him so he would pay another visit. Of course Jim wouldn't have gone to the celebration.

Jim Sees Hawk was an old man of the tribe who had never accepted the ways of the white man. He still wore his hair in braids and refused to speak English although he would listen to it. He lived in his tent on the creek, lonely as a badger. Everyone on the reservation called him Crazy Jim.

With the sound of the drums in the distance and the memory of the dances, Frankie had a sharp yearning to hear some stories of the old-time Sioux, and that was all that Jim Sees Hawk ever talked about.

# III

JIM SEES HAWK was happy to receive his young caller. He rose with the help of his walking stick and came forward with his hand held out. "How?" he asked in greeting.

"Fine," said Frankie in English. "How are you?"

Jim looked admiringly at the picture Frankie made on the spotted horse. "On horseback like a real Sioux boy," said Jim. "It is almost a moon since you have visited me."

"It isn't my horse," confessed Frankie. "It's Abel White Eagle's Spot. That's why I can't come often. You live so far from us and I don't have my own horse to ride."

He slid off the horse's back, happy that he could do that without help. He tied one of Spot's reins to the branch of a cottonwood.

"This will be the last time I'll see you for awhile," said Frankie. "School starts early this year. Next Monday the bus will come for us. Then we will be kept busy."

Jim savagely dug his walking stick into the ground. "Don't go back," he advised the boy. "The great buffalo herd is returning soon. The beasts will sweep over the prairie and drive the white ones into the sea. They will trample their stinkwagons underfoot and butt down the walls of those schools that try to teach our children white ways. Already I can hear the thunder of their hoofs."

Frankie couldn't hear anything but the sound of the locusts in the trees—as if they were shaking tiny deer-bone rattles.

He hung his head. "I have to go back to school," he said. "If I don't, Mr. Spooner or somebody will come after me."

"Whatever they teach you will be wrong," warned Jim. "Hai-yai! Soon the buffalo herd will be here."

Frankie remembered from his history book that long ago another Indian prophet had made such a promise. The buffalo hadn't returned but the white soldiers had come. Then there had been a terrible battle between the soldiers and the Indians. Many innocent Sioux women and children had been slaughtered. The old battlefield was pointed out with a marker, and the victims of the battle lay in a common grave up on a hill behind a church.

Jim Sees Hawk seemed to read his thoughts. "Long ago the buffalo herd was on its way back," he said, "but white soldiers came first and massacred the Sioux."

Frankie had heard the storekeeper and some of the white ranchers say that the Indians had been to blame for the battle because of their crazy ghost dances and threats.

"Perhaps it was like the fight at the basketball game in Little Axe," said Frankie. "Nobody knew for sure who was to blame."

Frankie had done a little fighting there himself. Nobody knew which team had started it, but both sides had been spoiling for a good fight. He supposed that was the way it had been in the old times at Wounded Knee.

The subject was suddenly changed by a furry

animal that came bounding up to them from the creek. It sat back on its haunches with its ringed tail stretched behind and peeped at Frankie through a black mask.

"That raccoon kit you found in the oak last spring," cried Frankie. "He's grown big. He's a half-grown coon now."

The raccoon had been away the last time Frankie had visited, sleeping in a tree or exploring the banks of the creek. The boy had almost forgotten about him.

The curious animal ambled over to Frankie and picked at the hole in the toe of his shoe to see what was inside.

"Watch this," said Jim. He pulled a strip of jerked meat from his belt and threw it to the raccoon. The creature examined it closely, passing it back and forth between the tiny paws that looked so human. Then it ran to the water bucket and began busily washing the jerky, still passing it from paw to paw under water.

"He sure is cute," said Frankie enviously. "I wish I had a pet coon."

The raccoon ate the wet jerky then came back,

stood on its hind legs and begged like a dog. Frankie remembered the lump of sugar left in the pocket of his jeans. He pulled it out and gave it to the raccoon. It ran back to the bucket and began washing the sugar. Then it looked down in surprise. The sugar lump had vanished in its paws. The raccoon looked into the bucket in a puzzled way. It put one paw in and felt all through the water. It put in both paws.

Frankie rolled on the ground with laughter. He thought that he had never seen anything so funny. Then he sat up and ran his fingers through his unruly scalplock. "Do you think you could catch me a little baby coon next spring?" he asked Jim.

The old man narrowed his eyes and looked far over the low hills dotted with scrubby pines. "Once the land belonged to the animals and the Indians," he said. "All were brothers. Now our land belongs to the white people and their stink-wagons and schools."

Frankie followed his eyes and saw that the sun was sinking over the hills. If he didn't hurry back, the White Eagles would miss their TV show. And Abel would want his horse again.

Jim Sees Hawk boosted Frankie up on the horse and untied the rein.

"I'll be ready for the buffalo herd," promised Frankie in order to please the old man even if he didn't believe his words. "The storekeeper is saving Crunchie box tops for me. When he gets ten, he'll send them in and they'll send me back a real Indian bow-and-arrow set. That's what it says on the box—'a genuine Indian bow with real feather-tipped arrows.'"

"Why don't you make your own bow and arrows?" asked Jim.

"They wouldn't be real Indian," explained Frankie. "These are handmade by Chief Lone Wolf. That's what it said on the box."

He started to turn the horse's head away.

"Wait!" cried Jim. He grabbed the raccoon and handed it to Frankie.

"A giveaway present," said Jim Sees Hawk. "So you don't forget that the Indian is big brother to wild things—not poor brother to the white man."

Frankie whooped with delight. He settled the raccoon in front of him and started Spot up the creek. If he followed it, he would get back to the park sooner. For a few minutes the raccoon kept perfectly still with surprise at this perch that moved over the land in such a bumpy way.

"I'm going to call you Little Brave," decided Frankie, and he cuddled the raccoon closer.

Then Little Brave grew restless. He explored the pocket of Frankie's jeans and the boy almost fell off trying to control the horse and the raccoon at the same time.

Suddenly the raccoon took it into his furry head to climb out on the branch in front of him.

The branch was Spot's neck. Before Frankie could stop him, he was on his way toward Spot's ears with his sharp little claws digging into the horse's mane.

Spot snorted and lowered his head. The raccoon dug his nails in tighter so he wouldn't fall off. The horse whinnied shrilly. It rose up on its hindlegs, pawing the air frantically. Frankie tried to grab a handful of mane but missed. He somersaulted head over Spot's tail to the ground.

The terrified raccoon dug his claws even deeper in his attempts to cling to the branch that was thrashing in such a windstorm. Spot went bucking down the creek. Little Brave couldn't hold on any longer. He sailed through the air and landed with a splash in the middle of the creek.

Spot vanished over the bank in the direction of the White Eagle ranch.

Little Brave sat up in the water with a surprised look on his sharp face. When Frankie appeared on the bank, the raccoon raised his paw to him. It was gripping a tiny frog. Then Little Brave looked as unconcerned as if he had dived off the horse for the sole purpose of catching the frog.

Frankie sat on the bank and laughed so hard that he didn't know whether he was aching from laughter or his fall. Then he remembered that he had nothing to laugh about. He wouldn't get back to the picnic in time for the White Eagles to make their TV show. And Abel's horse was surely on its way home instead of returning to its master.

Frankie knew that he wasn't a brave enough warrior to face the wrath of all the White Eagles. He took Little Brave in his arms and started the long walk across the prairie. The horse had sense enough to go home and he would do the same.

# IV

ON THE LONG WALK home, Frankie and Little Brave became better acquainted. Frankie learned that Little Brave had five rings around his tail, long whiskers like a cat and a hollow chest that just fitted over his arm. Little Brave found out that his new master had three cowlicks on his head, an ear hole on each side and soft skin inside the rip in his red shirt.

It was dark when Frankie arrived home, but the night sun was trying to shine as brightly as his daytime brother. The cabin was shot by his silver arrows. It looked cozy with the faint glow the kerosene lamp made through the window.

Grandma had moved her game indoors so that she would have more light. But she had cooked some beans and Alice had made biscuits although they were cold now.

Alice had done something else. She had washed her other blouse and a pair of socks that didn't have any holes so that she would be clean for school. She had also washed a shirt for Frankie and everything had dried fast on the barbed wire clothesline behind the cabin. Grandma had strung barbed wire so that she wouldn't have to bother with clothespins. Alice complained that it tore the clothes, especially if the wind was strong, but Grandma didn't think that holes in clothing mattered. "Nice clean holes," she called them.

When Frankie burst in with his raccoon, Alice was ironing the laundry with a flatiron Grandma had bought for cracking nuts.

"Where have you been?" demanded Alice. "Everybody was looking for you and the White Eagles came on home without you."

Frankie was relieved to learn that they had not waited for him. "Did Abel come home too?" he asked.

"No—what's that you've got there?" asked Alice, catching sight of Little Brave. "Where did you find it?"

Grandma Tomahawk looked at the raccoon

with interest too. "Make nice warm cap," she said.

Frankie tightened his arms around Little Brave protectively. "He's my *pet*," he answered. "Jim Sees Hawk gave him to me."

"So that's why you didn't come back," said Alice as she drew close to the raccoon. "Will he bite?"

"Not unless you bite him first," said Frankie.

Alice petted the animal gingerly. "He's cute," she agreed, "but he can't be dirty in this house. He's got to live outside."

"Dirty!" exclaimed Frankie huffily. "Raccoons are the cleanest animals in the world. They're always washing things."

To prove his words, he filled the washbasin with water from the bucket on the sink and set it down on the floor. Then he gave Little Brave one of the cold biscuits. The raccoon began swishing it around in the water until it was soggy. Then he sat down in the water himself and began to eat the biscuit.

Alice wasn't sure that she approved of him taking a bath in their washbasin, but she had to admit that he was cleanly.

Little Brave got out of the water and began looking about the room. He found a spoon then hurried to the basin to wash it. He poked his nose into corners and cracks. He found an old moccasin under the stove and promptly tried to wash that too.

"See how clean he is," declared Frankie. "I bet he doesn't have any germs at all."

Then Little Brave spied Grandma's coins on the ground when she turned all the way around. He loped over to them and sat down on his haunches. He picked up a coin, passed it back and forth between his paws then laid it down. During this time, the coin changed from an Indian to a buffalo. He picked up another coin, tried his teeth on it then changed it from a buffalo to an Indian.

Grandma giggled with glee. "Him play game with me," she cackled. "Him welcome in my house."

Grandma was so pleased with the new pet that she gave him a sip of her pancake syrup. Little Brave immediately grabbed the bottle from her, held it upside down and greedily drank the syrup.

"No, no," cried Grandma Tomahawk. She wrestled her syrup away from him. "You get sick and me get no syrup," she warned him. She put the bottle high up on a shelf.

When they got used to the antics of the raccoon, Frankie began questioning Alice again about the picnic in the grove.

"Did you say Abel didn't come home with you?" he asked.

"No," said Alice. "He was waiting for you so he could get his horse. The boys were going to have a race."

Frankie groaned. Alice went on with her news. Theresa Yellow Hawk fell in the creek and Amos White Deer got sick because he ate too much. Grandma Running Wolf tore the new purple shawl which had cost her sixty-five dollars, and the dogs got up on the table and ate all the leftover meat while everybody was watching the dancing. "It was lots of fun," finished Alice. "Why did you have to go off to see that superstitious old Indian?"

Frankie stayed around home Sunday so he wouldn't run into Abel White Eagle. He taught

Little Brave how to climb up on the sink and how to open the cupboard door although Alice didn't think that a raccoon should have that much knowledge.

Then Little Brave climbed on top of the squaw cooler. The dead branches must have made him homesick for the living trees because he vanished completely in the afternoon. Frankie was brokenhearted and thought that he was gone forever, but the raccoon came trotting from the direction of the cottonwood grove before supper.

Frankie felt unhappier about school than ever. He hated to think of being separated from Little Brave all day. But Alice was busy as a greenbug in a wheat field getting everything ready for Monday morning. She carefully laid out her clean blouse and socks on a chair. Then she took the washbasin away from Little Brave and scrubbed it hard in case a few germs had lived through all the washing he had done.

She stood in front of the mirror that made her face look crooked and began combing her straight black hair and dividing it into strands. Then she took some old rags she had also washed, wet a strand of hair and began winding it around the rag. When the hair was all wound, she took the rest of the rag and twisted it up over the hair.

Grandma watched the operation with interest. "Look real nice for school," she said. "You tie eagle feathers on ends, maybe."

Alice was disgusted. "I'm not going to wear my hair to school like *this*," she said. "I'm making curls. Gloria Jean White Eagle showed me this way to make curls if you can't buy a permanent." 1112713

Frankie looked at the rag bunches with a brotherly scorn. "I bet you won't have any curls," he said. "Your hair's like wire."

Alice ignored him. "I'm going to bed now," she announced, "so anybody who's going to stay in here will have to sit in the dark. Teacher said we should get plenty of sleep during the school year."

Grandma Tomahawk yawned and gathered up her coins. She made for the tent because that was her favorite bedroom until the real cold weather came. Frankie followed her. Sleeping in the tent was just like camping. Old carpets had been laid out on the ground for beds and there were soft pillows stacked at one side.

Little Brave started the night in the tent but he grew restless. Outside was the whole mysterious night with a full moon and strange sights and smells. He was getting old enough to think that it might be more fun to stay awake during the night and sleep in the daytime.

Frankie fell asleep so fast that he didn't even know that the raccoon had left. Alice's angry shrieks were his alarm clock next morning.

"I hate him! I hate him!" came the screaming voice. "If that old coon doesn't leave my things alone, I'll drown him in the bucket."

Frankie wondered what awful thing had happened. He soon found out. Little Brave had gone into the house during the night. He had pulled Alice's clean blouse and socks off the chair and had washed them in the bucket.

Alice pointed to the sodden lumps on the floor, one big one and two little ones. Then she threw herself on the bed and wept.

Frankie was sorry that Little Brave had ruined Alice's work, but he thought that she was making a big fuss over something which wasn't too important. However, he made Grandma promise to watch Little Brave during the day and keep him out of the house.

Grandma stoutly defended Little Brave because he played "five centses" with her. "You all time want wash, clean, wash," she told Alice. "Him do it."

Alice sponged her red eyes with the washcloth then put on the rumpled blouse she had been wearing. She slipped her bare feet into her run-down shoes. Then another great sorrow struck at her. When she unwrapped the curls and pulled out the rags, the long twists of hair slowly lengthened over her shoulders.

"They look like dying black snakes," she wailed.

Grandma tried to help her. "Put back inside rags," she suggested. "Real pretty and different that way."

But when Alice shed four more tears then began angrily brushing her hair with all the strength in her arm, it fell in a shower of soft waves. Even the funny mirror made her look pretty because of the wavy hair. Alice was satisfied. She even had an appetite for the pancakes Grandma made for breakfast. But Little Brave had to eat his outside because he hadn't been completely forgiven yet.

# V

FRANKIE AND ALICE waited at the head of the lane
for the school bus. Frankie hoped that it would
break down or something before it reached them.
But Alice was excited and kept running out into
the middle of the road.

At last they saw the big yellow bus coming
between the fences of barbed wire. Frankie
kicked at the dead sunflower bushes. The bus
stopped and he let Alice get on first, not through
politeness but because he was in no hurry to get
to school.

Hiram Burnt Hat as usual was driving. "Not
many kids this morning," he said. "Most of them
must have got back from the powwow too late."

Frankie fervently hoped that Abel White
Eagle was one of them because he hated to face

him. He stared out of the window when they approached the White Eagle ranch.

There were three car bodies rusting in the ragweeds and the house was closed in by a fence made of worn-out and blown-out auto tires. A TV antenna perched on the roof and an electric refrigerator was set up in the squaw cooler. Anyone could easily see that the White Eagles would not want to be old-time Indians.

Hiram Burnt Hat honked loudly but no one appeared. Frankie thought that he saw somebody asleep near the refrigerator.

The bus moved on, much to Frankie's relief. It stopped next for a woman and a very little girl waiting at an intersection. The child was weeping and clinging to her mother's hand. She didn't want to get on the bus. Hiram had to help pull her loose from her mother's hand.

"You will like school once you get there," assured her mother, "and Mama will be waiting right here for you when you come home on the bus."

Hiram Burnt Hat led the little girl to an empty seat then returned to the wheel. The bus lurched forward. The little girl sobbed into her fingers. Nobody paid any more attention to her—nobody but Alice Tomahawk. She left her seat and walked back to the unhappy child.

"What are you bawling about?" asked Alice. "Is this your first day at school?"

The child nodded with her fingers pressed to her face. Alice studied her short black hair. "You're Lily Her Many Horses, aren't you?" she asked.

The child nodded into her fingers again.

"Don't you want to go to school?" asked Alice.

Lily shook her head and sobbed harder.

"Every child has to go to school," said Alice. "You don't want to grow up to be an old bead sewer or spend all your life picking berries, do you?"

Lily shook her head again.

"Then you've got to get educated and civilized," said Alice. She slid into the seat beside Lily. "You aren't afraid of school, are you?" she asked in a gentler voice.

Lily kept on sobbing and nodded again.

"There's nothing to be afraid of," said Alice. "School is fun and the teachers are real nice. There's even a TV we get to watch sometimes." She pulled one hand away from Lily's face and held it tightly. "And I'm your friend so I'll take you to your room when we get there and if you have any trouble, you can come to me. I'm Alice Tomahawk."

Lily stopped crying. She dried her eyes with the sleeve of her blouse. She looked up at Alice with a sudden smile.

"You look pretty when you smile," said Alice. "You should smile all the time."

The bus rumbled and rattled on through the tiny village of one store and four houses, up the winding road to the Little Axe school.

The school looked like a ranch with its windmill and many small outbuildings. There were two white frame school buildings, which needed paint, a teacher's cottage and the principal's house enclosed by a barbed-wire fence. On the other side of the school buildings was the mess hall and behind that the log community cabin where the parents met.

The playground was weedy in some places, rocky in others and dusty in all, but it had a well-worn slide and a merry-go-round. All around stretched the brown prairie with low hills crimping the horizons, like a great scorched pie crust.

The children trickled out of the bus to find Mr. and Mrs. Spooner waiting to receive them on this first day of school. Mr. Spooner was a kindly man with thick glasses and a bald head. Although Mrs. Spooner's hair was gray, she didn't look like anybody's grandmother. Her short hair was worn in neat waves and her figure was slim in the tailored suit. Alice would have been surprised to know that Mrs. Spooner was as old as Grandma Tomahawk.

Mrs. Spooner could be very severe if there was need for it, and the children feared her more than they did Mr. Spooner. Although he was principal, he also taught the second and third grades in one of the cottages. Mrs. Spooner taught fifth and sixth grades in the other cottage, and that was the only comfort Frankie felt in not having been promoted to fifth grade.

The other teachers would be strangers. Like Lily, they would be experiencing their first day at the Little Axe school. Alice was curious to see her new teacher but she had to think of Lily.

She took the child by the hand again and led her to the Spooners. "I'm so glad school is starting," she said to them. "This is Lily Her Many Horses and she has never been to school before. May I take her to her room?"

"Certainly," said Mrs. Spooner. "That is very thoughtful of you, Alice."

Alice felt a glow all over because she loved the warmth of praise well deserved. She hurried to the nearest cottage.

The other children greeted the Spooners, some more politely and enthusiastically than others. Frankie said, "Good morning, Mr. and Mrs. Spooner," then made for the farthest cottage.

He was surprised at sight of the new teacher who had come to teach the fourth grade. She was young and blonde and pretty.

"I'm Miss Anna Hansen," she told the children, "and all summer I have been looking forward to coming here."

Miss Hansen had eyes like bluebells and hair like goldenrod, thought Alice, deciding to make up a poem about her new teacher. She thought Miss Hansen was the most beautiful person she had ever seen and that she would study twice as hard as ever and never do anything wrong.

But Frankie couldn't forgive Miss Hansen for being his teacher this year when he should have been in fifth grade.

There was new furniture in the schoolroom and the children thought the pale yellow and chrome desks with their undershelves and chrome chairs looked too pretty to use. What boy would dare carve his initials on one of them this year? But the walls needed painting and Frankie had noticed that the screen door at the entry was still broken.

The desks were arranged in groups of four and Billie Afraid of Hawk did not mind sitting with Lester Yellow Hawk and Myrna Flying Hawk. But Amos White Deer didn't want to be grouped with Helen Never Misses Shot and Linda Running Wolf because they were girls.

Each child knew that the Spooners had put much hard work on the buildings themselves but the parents had been asked to do the painting and to repair the doors. Each child was ashamed that his parents had done nothing to help. But he was proud of the beautiful new desks. And the PTA ladies had made checked pink-and-white curtains for the windows.

Books were passed out, a few new but most old. Frankie scowled at his old ones because he had used them before.

After they had filled out cards with their names and addresses, the children were given an arithmetic review test. Miss Hansen wrote the numbers on the greenboard.

"Now suppose you had four horses," she slowly supposed. "Then you sold one horse for $20.50, another for $30.75, a third for $35.25 and the fourth for $23.37," she continued, writing the numbers in a column with the yellow chalk. "How much would you receive for your horses?"

All the groups of black heads bowed over the papers. Myron Two Bears chewed on his pencil. Myrna Flying Hawk raised her hand. "Do we add?" she asked, because Myrna was one of those pupils who don't pay attention.

Frankie stuck out his underlip after he had copied the numbers. Then he made a big O below, as big as a sparrow's egg. If he had four horses he wouldn't sell any of them so he wouldn't get any money. He would have his own ranch and start buying cattle.

Miss Hansen gave them some more problems but Frankie missed two because he had his mind on his ranch with the horses. If he had four horses, he would have one more than Mr. White Eagle.

When Miss Hansen asked for a volunteer to gather up the papers for her, Alice waved her hand so wildly that she was chosen for the task. Then the teacher sat down to look over the papers after giving the children some silent reading in their books. Frankie peeped at her from the corner of his right eye. He knew when she reached his paper.

"Frank Tomahawk," said Miss Hansen. Frankie looked up sullenly. "You have not done the

horse problem," she said. "Why did you put a zero as the sum? Even a first grader would know better than that."

Frankie pouted and slouched lower in his seat.

"Answer me, Frank," ordered Miss Hansen, but he didn't.

When the bell rang for recess, Miss Hansen kept Frankie in. He waited for her to give him a good scolding or send him to Mrs. Spooner, but Miss Hansen's voice was low and even.

"Work the first five problems on page 23," she said in a very matter-of-fact voice.

Frankie bent over the arithmetic book with all his attention. He wanted to show Miss Hansen that he wasn't really stupid. She was the stupid one for expecting a Sioux boy to sell all his horses —and for such silly prices at that. He tried to think out each problem carefully because he knew that little traps had been set in them.

"What did you do during vacation?" Miss Hansen suddenly asked him in a friendly tone.

"Nothing," said Frankie.

"Didn't you go camping or ride horseback?" she asked.

Frankie didn't say anything because he thought that the question had already been answered.

"What do you like to do?" tried Miss Hansen.

"Nothing," said Frankie. How could he figure out the arithmetic problems if she was going to keep talking to him?

But she suddenly ambushed him with the question, "Do you have any pets? A dog or a calf maybe."

He looked up from his desk with his eyes sparkling. "I've got a raccoon," he said. "A real smart coon that can play games and wash clothes."

"How interesting and different!" exclaimed Miss Hansen. "When I was a little girl I had a banty rooster. He used to follow me all over the farm and eat corn from my hand. But a raccoon must be much more fun than a rooster. Perhaps you will bring your raccoon to school someday."

Frankie realized that Miss Hansen and her rooster had tricked him into conversation. He dropped his head.

"I called my rooster Perky," continued his teacher. "What is your raccoon's name?"

Frankie was angry with Miss Hansen for her

trickery. He was angry because she was so pretty and had such a friendly voice. It would be so much easier to be sullen with Mrs. Spooner although the punishment would have been greater. "Spot," he finally answered, feeling he was having his revenge by giving the wrong name for his raccoon.

"My, that's an odd name for a raccoon," said Miss Hansen. "They don't have spots, do they?"

Frankie refused to say any more. If Miss Hansen didn't know what a raccoon looked like, he wasn't going to tell her. And he wasn't going to bring his coon to school for her to find out.

Before lunch Miss Hansen gave them a talk about the importance of cleanliness and good health. She pointed to the water basin with the big sign over it, WASH YOUR HANDS. She pointed to the poster on the cloakroom door, DON'T HELP GERMS. WASH YOUR HANDS. She called attention to the notices in the library books, ARE YOUR HANDS CLEAN?

Frankie thought that teacher must think that they were raccoons. How pleased she would be with Little Brave if he ever came to school. But he wouldn't because Frankie wouldn't bring him.

Before they boarded the bus to go home, Mr. Spooner came into the room and reminded the pupils to remind their parents about the school walls and the broken doors. He particularly told Myron Two Bears that he wanted to see his mother because she was president of the PTA.

# VI

THE YELLOW BUS was waiting to take the children home. Some of them raced for it with the chance to get the best seats by the windows. Others ran for the playground and the chance to have a last slide or whirl on the merry-go-round before the ride home.

Hiram Burnt Hat honked impatiently. He thrust his head out of the window. "You kids come on," he bawled. "I got to get to my farm and cows."

"Children," called Mrs. Spooner, clapping her hands. "Don't loiter. Get on the bus. Your parents will be waiting for you."

Frankie knew that Grandma wouldn't be waiting for him and Alice especially. But he went flying down the slide then ran for the bus. He wished he had gone there first because all the good seats were taken. He had to run the gauntlet to get to an empty place. Amos White Deer and Lester Yellow Hawk were wrestling in the aisle. Then Myron Two Bears put out his leg and tripped him, and Billie Afraid of Hawk took a swipe at his scalplock as he went by.

Hiram made the motor growl and slowly edged the bus forward. At last everyone was inside. School was over for the day. There was the whole glorious free evening.

Alice Tomahawk was sitting beside Lily Her Many Horses again. She reached for the piece of paper in the child's hand.

"Let's see what you did today," she said encouragingly.

Lily tried to press the paper flat because it was crumpled from carrying. "I crayoned a picture," she said proudly.

Alice looked at the crayon picture critically. "It's real good," she said. "What is it?"

Lily looked surprised. "It's our house," she said, "and that's the sun over the roof and down in the corner is Papa's old car—the one that was in the wreck. He put the wheels on our wagon."

Alice brought the picture closer to her eyes. She remembered that the Her Many Horses' house was pink with a green roof. "You ought to have your father fix the chimney," she said. "And why doesn't he take that dead car away?"

Lily looked more surprised. "We keep our chickens in the car," she explained. "That's a chicken near it."

"Are your chickens purple?" asked Alice.

"I wanted to use that crayon for something," said Lily.

Her underlip began to tremble. Alice was afraid that she would begin crying on the bus again. She tried to think of something nice to say about the picture. "The colors are beautiful," she decided. "I've never seen such a red sun or such a green roof. I bet your mother will be proud when she sees your picture. She'll probably hang it up on the wall."

There was a wistful note in Alice's voice because Grandma Tomahawk never took any interest in her or Frankie's schoolwork. "Look like bird tracks," was all the old woman would ever say about a school paper. Perhaps if Grandma had praised some of Frankie's work, he would have wanted to study harder. Alice decided that Lily shouldn't lose interest in school because of any lack of praise.

"I bet you're real smart in school," she told Lily. "I bet you'll be a great painter someday."

"And have my own crayons?" asked Lily in awe.

"Crayons are for school," said Alice. "You'll probably have jars and jars of wet paints and lots of brushes."

Lily smiled her prettiest smile. She thought that Alice meant that when she grew up she would be able to paint a house all by herself like her father had done.

The ride home on the bus always seemed longer than the one that brought them to school, and Frankie was suffering to get home and find out how Little Brave had behaved all day.

He was angry at Amos White Deer when he threw his shoe out of the window and the bus had to stop and wait for him to run back for it. But he wished that Hiram would stop and let them look at the whitetail deer that was grazing in a pasture with some cattle.

The deer took fright at something. It threw back its antlers and went bounding across the field as if its legs were made of rubber. An easy bound lifted it over the fence and another carried it across the road. Hiram Burnt Hat had to jam on the brakes as the deer cut across in front of the bus.

He stuck his head out of the window. "Can't you see we've got the right of way?" he shouted to the graceful creature.

Then they saw what had frightened the deer. It was Abel White Eagle running across the field and madly waving to the bus. Like the deer he cleared the fence with one bound, but he ripped his jeans as he did so.

Hiram waited for him impatiently. "Jiminy!" he exclaimed. "Everything's on the run today. All running the wrong way. Hope my cows haven't got tired of waiting for me and run off too."

All the children laughed but Frankie. He had hoped that the driver wouldn't wait for Abel.

But the boy made it to the bus in no time although he was panting and his face was red.

"Why are you going home on the bus when you didn't go to school on it?" demanded Hiram.

Abel hesitated and looked around for a vacant seat. "I got to go home before I can go to school," he said. "I'm just getting back from the celebration."

"Thought maybe you'd moved off the reservation," said Hiram because he always had to have the last word with the children. Otherwise, he thought that they wouldn't respect him.

The seat across the aisle from Frankie was empty but Abel didn't take it. He glared at Frankie as if he were a snake lying in the road then brushed past him.

"Hi, Billie!" he shouted, giving the boy in back a friendly punch. "Hi, Lester!" But he acted as if there was no Frankie Tomahawk on the school bus.

Frankie felt miserable. He didn't see why Abel had to act like that to his best friend. He could have asked Frankie for an explanation of why he hadn't brought the horse back. He might know that something had happened. Frankie could have been killed in his fall from the horse. Then Abel would have been sorry.

On the other hand, Frankie had the uncomfortable feeling that it was just as easy for him to explain as for Abel to ask. He pondered over the thought as the bus drove past gullies with pink fluted walls. At last he slowly turned around.

"Hi, Abel!" he greeted him. Perhaps Abel hadn't really seen him. Perhaps he wouldn't have to explain anything.

But Abel only scowled. "Who's he?" he rudely asked his seat partner. "I've never seen that brushy head before."

Frankie tried to flatten his scalplock. "I'm sorry about Spot," he said. "He threw me off and then he ran home. And I had to walk home."

Abel turned all the way around in the seat so that his back faced Frankie. But having started his apology, Frankie was stubbornly determined that his friend had to accept it.

"I should have gone back to the grove and told you," he continued. "But—but—well, I didn't. I walked home instead."

Abel brushed at his ears as if Frankie's words were mosquitoes whining around them.

"It was the raccoon scared Spot," went on Frankie. "When the raccoon climbed out on his neck, it scared Spot so bad he threw me."

At this interesting information, Abel couldn't overlook Frankie any longer. "A raccoon?" he asked, turning around. "Did it jump out of a tree on Spot?"

Frankie knew that the misunderstanding with Abel was over. "He's my pet raccoon," said Frankie. "Jim Sees Hawk gave him to me."

"Have you still got him?" asked Abel. "Can I see him?"

He came to Frankie and leaned against his seat to show that he was willing to enter into conversation with him now.

But first Abel had to air his own grievances. He had stayed on at the celebration even though he had received word that Spot was at home. Then he had spent the night with the Standing Bears because they had promised to drive him home next day. But Mr. Standing Bear's truck wouldn't run because there wasn't any more gasoline in it. So Abel had thought of walking down the road and waiting for the school bus to catch up with him. Then he had seen the deer and had gone into the field for a closer look. And if it hadn't been for the deer running in front of the bus, he probably would have missed it.

"But I want to get off at the White Horse store and buy a Coke," said Abel, jingling some coins in his pocket. "You get off with me and I'll buy you one."

Frankie considered this although he was in such a hurry to get back to Little Brave. "Will you buy my raccoon a Coke too?" he asked Abel. "I'll let you play with him."

Abel thought this over. "You never bought Spot a Coke," he accused.

"I gave him a lump of sugar," Frankie reminded him. "And I would have given him another but I gave it to Little Brave."

"Who's Little Brave?" asked Abel.

"The raccoon," said Frankie. "He's got to have a name, doesn't he?"

"Okay," decided Abel. "Hey, here's the store now. Whoa, Hiram!"

# VII

THE STORE was the heart of the community on that part of the reservation. It wasn't only a store. It was club, newspaper and restaurant for the people who lived within many miles. It was home for Joe Dust Maker because he sat on the steps all day long. Although Joe hadn't gone past the sixth grade, one of his sons was a fine doctor in California. Joe could have gone to California, too, but he loved the White Horse store more than any other place in the world.

Outside of the store was the big gasoline pump and without that the ranchers and car owners would have been as helpless as old-time Sioux without prairie grass for their horses.

It was really a small building covered with green tar-paper shingles, but it was bursting with all the things that the reservation people needed.

*63*

To Frankie and Abel, it was a treasure house of pop, candies, knives and chewing gum. But the most breath-taking of all was the showcase of Indian handicraft. Frankie loved to lean on the case and stare at the beaded moccasins, eagle-feather headdresses and buckskin clothing. With such garments available, he couldn't understand why the Sioux people went around wearing faded cotton dresses, dull jeans and clumpy factory shoes. Of course he wore jeans and an old faded shirt because the prices marked on the handmade articles were more than the Tomahawks could afford.

Some older men and women were gathered around Joe Dust Maker, chatting about crops and cattle and what the government should do to help them.

Frankie and Abel politely returned their greetings then went through the rusty screen door. There were a number of women inside doing their last shopping for the day. Two men were drinking pop near the giant refrigerator and some women were comparing prices of cold cuts in the open case.

Frankie saw that the notice about the park celebration was still tacked on the door—also the notice for the celebration of the year before, although it was torn and hung by one tack.

Mr. Kirk, the storekeeper, was gossiping with Mrs. Hollow Horn while he weighed her hamburger.

"Yeah, droughts in the summer and blizzards in the winter," said Mr. Kirk. "Washington ought to do something for the farmers. This is a little over two pounds."

"The grasshoppers was bad this year," put in Mrs. Kirk, who was part Sioux although she had gray eyes and light brown hair. "I'll almost be glad to see winter come."

Mr. Kirk caught sight of Frankie's scalplock over the counter. "How, Chief!" he called. "Your bow-and-arrow set came. Just in time for hunting season. Maybe you'll be able to bag some pheasants."

Frankie was so excited about the package that he almost forgot about the Cokes. But Abel made Mr. Kirk give them the bottles before he gave Frankie the long, tightly-wrapped parcel.

"You be sure to tell your grandma they're going to give out surplus food to the needy Indians next Wednesday," Mr. Kirk informed Frankie.

Frankie nodded. He wouldn't forget. He knew that if they were going to give out free food Grandma would want to be a needy Indian. He wished they would give the needy Indians candy and cookies instead of rice and beans and stuff like that. They still had an unopened bag of rice left in the cupboard at home because none of the Tomahawks was needy enough to eat rice.

The boys went outside and lolled on the ground to drink their Cokes. Abel blew bubbles into his bottle but Frankie was too interested in his package to play with his Coke.

He had quite a job unwrapping the package and knocked his bottle over, spilling most of the drink. The people who had wrapped the package must have wanted to be sure it would be safe in train wreck, flood or fire. Abel finally pulled out his knife and slit the heavy paper.

"Hai-yai!" cried Frankie with shining eyes. "What a bow!"

It was painted with all the colors that Lily Her Many Horses had used in her crayon picture. And there was a festoon of ribbons on one end. The bow would have astonished an old-time Indian. There were three arrows but the feathers were cut out of paper and the points were blunt.

"That's some bow!" admitted Abel enviously. "I wonder how Chief Lone Wolf thought about tying all these ribbons on it? They'll get in your way when you try to shoot."

Frankie handled the bow reverently. To think that Chief Lone Wolf had fashioned it for him —an unknown boy on a reservation in South Dakota.

Another boy joined Frankie and Abel to look at the bow. "Did you buy it in the store?" he asked. "Who made it?"

"It came through the mail from Chief Lone Wolf," said Frankie impressively. "He makes them for people who eat Crunchies."

The new arrival admiringly ran his hand over the bow. He snapped the ribbons. He squinted at the inner side of the bow. "It says something inside," he called their attention.

Abel looked down quickly. "It says 'made in Japan,'" he read.

Frankie read the printing too. "I wonder what Chief Lone Wolf is doing in Japan," he pondered.

"He probably went there with a dance band," suggested Abel. "Like Chief Running Deer took his to Arizona and Europe."

"Perhaps he lives there," said Frankie. "Lots of our people leave the reservation and go to California or down to Nebraska."

Frankie fitted an arrow into the bow. He sighted along the arrow to the gas pump. He pulled the string and z-z-z-t the arrow flew through the air and hit Joe Dust Maker between the shoulders.

Joe pretended to be badly wounded. He groaned and rubbed his back. Then he picked up the arrow and looked at it. "What kind of bird got feathers like this?" he asked Frankie.

"It's probably a Japanese bird," said Abel. "A Japanese Indian made Frankie's bow."

Frankie was proud of all the attention that his bow and arrows were receiving. But he was afraid that someone might break them before he had a chance to use them much himself. The bow didn't look very strong and the arrows looked even flimsier.

He and Abel took turns shooting at doves and pheasants as they walked down the dusty road, but the birds didn't act very frightened. They flew a short distance away then returned to forage by the roadside.

By the time the boys reached the Tomahawk cabin, one of the paper feathers had parted from its shaft.

Grandma Tomahawk was squatting in the doorway of the cabin, braiding her hair. She looped the braids over her shoulders then pulled a shampoo net neatly over the crown of her head. She patted the faded purple dress that didn't fit her anywhere and changed the position of two safety pins on the bodice. She touched the lobes of her ears to make sure that the colored glass earrings that she had bought at the store were still there. Then she settled back comfortably and folded her arms. She was ready for the evening.

Abel politely stepped up and shook her hand.

70

"How!" greeted Grandma. "Your papa and mama well? Everything good?"

"They're all well and good," said Abel, "but the antelopes are getting into the sorghum field. Papa says he is going to shoot them."

Grandma Tomahawk whistled through the space between her teeth. "All time antelopes, drought, grasshoppers, blizzards," she said.

There was a commotion inside the cabin and Little Brave scooted out followed by a brush.

"How can I write a poem with him trying to write it, too?" cried Alice's angry voice. She appeared behind Grandma, pencil in hand.

"Gosh, he's real tame," said Abel when Little Brave came to him and tried to untie his shoestring.

Abel pried the top off the Coke bottle and gave it to Little Brave. The raccoon held the bottle between his paws and drained it quickly.

"Him got new game," cried Grandma. "New hide-and-find game."

She clucked to Little Brave in Sioux. The raccoon dropped the empty bottle and ran to Grandma. She handed him one of her coins and he went running past Alice into the cabin. Then he came back, sat on his haunches in front of Grandma and purred deeply in his throat.

"Him hide five centses in coffeepot," laughed Grandma. "Him all time hide in coffeepot." She led the boys into the cabin and triumphantly took the coffeepot from the sink. There were several nickels in it. Grandma shook the pot, clinking the coins. Then she gave Little Brave a swallow of pancake syrup as a reward for his cleverness.

"He better not put any of my things in the coffeepot," warned Alice. "And he better stay outside if he's going to get sick drinking all that sweet stuff. Why do you spend all your time banging that coffeepot, Grandma, and playing with the raccoon?" she continued impatiently. "Why don't you use that money to make some pretty curtains for our house? Why don't you buy some nice rugs like the White Eagles'?"

Grandma blinked her bright eyes at Alice. "Sometime," she promised.

"Sometime!" exclaimed Alice. "Sometime we'll live in a big clean house. Sometime we'll have nice new clothes instead of what comes out of the mission boxes. Sometime we'll have a garden and some chickens. And sometime it'll snow in August and there'll be a drought in January."

Alice's remark about the mission boxes reminded Frankie of the storekeeper's message.

"They're giving out food to the needy Indians next Wednesday," he told Grandma Tomahawk.

"Rice?" asked Grandma with little interest. "All time white men grow too much rice and make poor Indian eat it."

"Perhaps butter too," said Frankie, "and flour."

"Me go see," said Grandma.

"You're not a needy Indian, Grandma," said Alice. "You've got money if you'd spend it instead of playing with it. You could buy your own butter and flour and some goods to make us pretty curtains."

Grandma Tomahawk sat down in the midst of her nickels. "Me poor old Indian," she mumbled. "Talk bad English. Dress like Indian. Eat like Indian. Not like rice."

Abel tried to be polite. "Papa says you're a real old-time Sioux, Grandma Tomahawk," he told her. "He says there aren't many like you left."

Alice gave him a cold look. "Who wants to be a leftover Sioux?" she asked. "We're Americans. We're citizens. That's what teacher says. Teacher says we're all born free and equal in the United States and we can make ourselves whatever we want. All we need is ambition and to work hard."

Grandma's old eyes had a remembering look. "Me work hard," she said. "Build cabin with my man. Dig corn. Skin deer. Carry water and wood. Teacher Says work hard like that?"

"She's *educated*," said Alice. "Teacher says she waited on tables to put herself through college."

Abel White Eagle was afraid that he hadn't made things any better in the Tomahawk family. "I've got to go," he said. "Here I am playing with your Little Brave and I haven't seen Spot yet. I bet Spot thinks I went to Japan with Chief Lone Wolf."

"I'll see you on the bus tomorrow," said Frankie.

Abel cackled like a cock pheasant to show what he thought about the bus and school.

74

# VIII

THE CLUSTER of ribbons on the Japanese bow did not interfere with Frankie's shooting skill very long. The first time Little Brave found the bow unguarded, he pulled the ribbons loose. He carried them off into the cottonwoods and dropped them into an owl's hole.

Frankie never found the ribbons and Alice mourned because she could have worn them in her hair. Frankie did not mind the loss but even he was angered at the raccoon when he found the busy little creature chewing on the wood of the bow. He had to be more careful now so that it was hung out of a raccoon's reach. He knew how Alice had felt when Little Brave had washed the floor with her clothing.

A few days later Abel White Eagle thought up a wonderful idea for the bow and arrows. It was such a clever idea that he wondered why he hadn't thought of it before. When he and Frankie got off the school bus in the morning, they could sneak around the community cabin, follow the draw out of sight and go antelope hunting in Hiram Burnt Hat's pasture. Hiram had mentioned during one ride that there were some antelopes grazing regularly with his cows.

A shelter belt of trees ran along one side of the pasture to break the wind. It would make a grand hiding place from which to shoot antelopes. Abel would sharpen the arrowheads with his knife because he thought that they were too blunt even to kill grasshoppers.

Of course he and Frankie would have to be careful that they did shoot antelopes instead of Hiram's cows. They would go back to school in time for a bountiful lunch in the dining room then run off again and not return until it was time for the bus to take the pupils home. Their only problem would be how to get their slain antelopes home.

Frankie had his bow and arrows with him as he impatiently waited for the bus next morning.

"Why are you so worried about getting to school on time?" asked Alice suspiciously.

"I want to practice my spelling some more before the test, Little Big Eyes," replied Frankie. The spelling test was one reason why this free day on the prairie would be so delightful.

Alice looked even more suspicious. Perhaps Frankie was eager to show his bow and arrows to Miss Hansen and the class, but why hadn't he brought them to school before?

When they climbed aboard the bus, Frankie made for a back seat because he thought it would be easier for him and Abel to sneak away if they got off last.

But when Abel stepped on, he dropped into a front seat, scanned the bus then violently beckoned for Frankie to join him.

Frankie shook his scalplock and motioned Abel to come back to the seat that he was saving for him. After a duel of waving arms and beckoning hands, Abel won. Frankie unwillingly joined him in the front seat.

"We could get away better if we sat in back," Frankie insisted.

"But we'll be able to talk to Hiram up here," said Abel. "We can ask him more about the antelopes."

Hiram obligingly answered their questions. The last time he had been out to the pasture, the antelopes were there again. You didn't think a barbed-wire fence and some wind-blown trees would keep antelopes out, did you?

"You going to shoot them with that fancy bow?" asked Hiram.

Frankie's heart skipped to think that Hiram had guessed their plan. He felt better when he realized that the driver was only joking.

Someone stepped out in the road ahead and waved for the bus to stop. It was such a large figure even at that distance that it couldn't have belonged to anyone but Mrs. Two Bears, hitching a ride like Grandma Tomahawk often did. But why wasn't Myron with her?

Hiram obligingly stopped and Mrs. Two Bears heavily climbed the steps. Her arms were always full of notebooks and big brown envelopes because she was president of the PTA. She was a very stout woman who prided herself on being quite a modern Sioux. Her short hair was frizzed with a permanent and she wore a clean, stiffly starched cotton dress. The turquoise earrings bobbing about her neck proved that she had traveled on other reservations than Sioux. She had gone all the way to the Navajo reservation in Arizona. And not as a dancer but as delegate to an inter-tribal meeting.

Mrs. Two Bears studied the narrow aisle. The children measured her size with their eyes. Everyone realized that Mrs. Two Bears would not be able to get to a back seat. Frankie and Abel did not want to give up their seats because they hadn't asked Hiram yet at what time the antelopes usually grazed with his cows.

Two children across the aisle offered their seats to Mrs. Two Bears. She sank down with a sigh of relief and all of the leather cushioning disappeared under her and her load. After a few minutes of silence to catch her breath, Mrs. Two Bears began looking around. Her attention rested on Frankie and Abel who sat across from her.

"Good morning, boys," she greeted them. "Are your parents coming to PTA this year?"

Frankie and Abel wriggled nervously.

"I guess so," replied Abel, trying to satisfy Mrs. Two Bears so that she would leave him alone. "They belonged last year but they didn't go to the meetings unless there was something to eat."

"Will Grandma Tomahawk join?" Mrs. Two Bears asked Frankie. "We missed her last year."

Frankie began combing his scalplock with his fingers. "She isn't parents," he said at last. "She's just our grandmother."

"Then it is even more important for her to belong to the PTA," said Mrs. Two Bears firmly. "We need grandmothers as well as mothers. They have had the experience of raising two families of children."

"I'll tell her," said Frankie without enthusiasm. "Where's Myron?" he asked. He was annoyed because his classmate wasn't present to talk to his own mother.

"He is sick in bed," answered Mrs. Two Bears,

"but I gave him some books to study so he won't miss out on his schooling."

Mrs. Two Bears began asking the boys about their schoolwork. "You're a repeater, aren't you?" she questioned Frankie.

There it was—the hated word. Mrs. Spooner had used it only twice and Miss Hansen had never made any mention of Frankie's being kept back.

Frankie wished that Mrs. Two Bears had missed the bus. It was a relief to reach the school grounds. The boys rose to make a dash for the door but Mrs. Two Bears locked her fingers around Frankie's arm.

"I'm going to your room so I can get the lesson assignments for Myron," she told him. "You can go with me and carry my things."

The boys looked at each other miserably.

"We have to go see Mr. Spooner first," said Abel with his eyes brightening.

"That's all right," said Mrs. Two Bears agreeably. "I'll go with you."

The brightness left Abel's eyes. "I guess we really don't have to see him first," he said.

Frankie descended the bus steps with lagging feet. Mrs. Two Bears' books and envelopes were in his arms, his bow was slung over his shoulder and his arrows were clutched to his chest. Slowly he and Abel followed Mrs. Two Bears' great

figure to the farthest cottage. Frankie had a wild desire to throw the books across the playground and sprint for the community cabin. But he could not find enough courage for that because Mrs. Two Bears' size was so forbidding.

At the cottage the two boys parted. Abel made for the entrance on the right because it led into the fifth and sixth grade room. Frankie and his captor went up the steps of the left side door to the fourth grade. But before they went in, Frankie gave Abel a savage scowl which plainly said, "I told you we should have sat in back."

He followed Mrs. Two Bears' stiffly starched dress into the classroom. The glorious day which he and Abel had planned was ruined. There would be no antelope hunt in Hiram Burnt Hat's pasture. There would be only a long, dull day of arithmetic problems, reading and the spelling test.

Mrs. Two Bears was bad medicine, as the old-time Indians called anything which brought them ill luck.

# IX

FRANKIE was freed from Mrs. Two Bears at last, but his freedom had come too late. He was now Miss Hansen's prisoner. He stuffed his bow and arrows in the shelf under his desk and tried to study his spelling lesson since he would be present for the test. He hadn't put any work on the words because he had thought he wouldn't be in the classroom to write them.

The words looked so long and difficult, but Frankie realized that he had often seen them in books. He certainly used "buffalo" himself.

A terrifying thought gripped the boy. Perhaps he would never pass into the fifth grade. Perhaps he would always be in the fourth grade until he was a grown man who couldn't fit at the desk.

If he had been born long ago, he wouldn't have had such a worry. If he had been born when the

Sioux were mighty warriors and hunters, he would have been out on the plains shooting buffalo instead of spelling them.

Frankie began to dream. He fingered his bow lovingly. His mind was far out on the endless prairies where the Indians once pitched their tepees and followed the b-u-f-f-a-l-o.

Miss Hansen's voice brought him back to the classroom. "Frank Tomahawk, what are you playing with under your desk?" she asked.

Frankie was shocked by more than the swift return to the fourth grade. Miss Hansen would take his bow away from him as she had taken Myrna Flying Hawk's comic book. She would throw it into the trash can and have it burned.

He looked up at her with desperate black eyes. "It's a bow," he answered sullenly.

"Bring it to me," commanded Miss Hansen. Frankie didn't move. "I said 'bring it to me,' Frank," commanded Miss Hansen with her blue eyes flashing like heat lightning.

Frankie twisted from side to side then obeyed. He stood near her desk and gripped the bow defiantly. He had made up his mind that he wasn't

*85*

going to let Miss Hansen throw it away. He held to it tightly.

Miss Hansen studied Frankie's tense figure. Her eyes dropped to the bow and she looked at it for a few minutes. Then she spoke. "It is nice that you brought the bow to show the class," she said softly. "I hope this will encourage other pupils to bring educational things for all of us to see."

She ran her finger along the string and tapped the wood. "I have never seen such a pretty bow," she said. "The class and I would like to hear about it. Has it been in your family for a long time or did you make it yourself?"

Frankie was taken back. It seemed to him that Miss Hansen was always fooling him. He felt as disarmed as if she had taken the bow away from him.

"It's a real Indian bow made by Chief Lone Wolf," said Frankie. "He made it while he was in Japan."

Miss Hansen was surprised. "Are you sure of that, Frank?" she asked. "Japan is a long way off —in Asia."

But Frankie had his proof. "It says so," he informed her. "It says 'made in Japan.'"

He handed the bow to Hiss Hansen. She read the printed words. A little smile curled the corners of her lips. "It is a very fine bow," she said, "and such pretty colors! Let's hang it over the shelf here and start a display of Sioux crafts." So saying, she went to the shelf, took down a "wash your hands" poster and hung Frankie's bow on its nail. "Does anyone else have any interesting Indian article he can bring to school to add to the display?" asked Miss Hansen. "We should be proud of our heritage and the work done by our ancestors."

"I've got some arrowheads," said Billy Afraid of Hawk. "I found them over by the cutbanks."

"I'll bring my beaded moccasins," offered Linda Running Wolf.

"We have an old pipe," boasted Helen Never Misses Shot. "It's like one in the museum in Rapid City."

"We've got a picture of my father when he was a baby," said Myrna Flying Hawk because she hadn't been paying much attention and thought that Miss Hansen wanted anything from home.

"Is he on a cradleboard?" asked Miss Hansen.

"No," answered Myrna, "he's on his stomach."

"Perhaps you could find something else," suggested her teacher. "Something that was handmade by a Sioux craftsman."

"We have a potato smasher that Papa made," insisted Myrna, "and he's a Sioux."

Alice had nothing to donate to the display because she had always scorned Indian handicraft.

Frankie had mixed feelings about the project which he had begun. He wouldn't be able to go antelope hunting as long as his bow was in the display. But he was proud that his teacher had admired it so much.

"There are three arrows that go with it," said Frankie. "I'll get them out of my desk."

The arrows were of no use without the bow. He felt more generous about giving them up.

While Miss Hansen was trying to arrange the arrows artistically on the shelf, Mr. Spooner came into the room with Mrs. Two Bears. He was politely carrying her notebooks and envelopes.

"Mrs. Two Bears would like to speak to the children about the PTA," he said to Miss Hansen. "The first meeting will be held two weeks from today and we want to stimulate interest among the parents."

Mrs. Two Bears faced the groups of desks. "All of your parents should join the PTA," she told the occupants. "This first meeting of the year will be interesting and stimulating."

Mr. Spooner broke in. "To whom does this school belong?" he asked the children.

They wrinkled their brows and some of them nibbled on their pencils. This question had never been asked them before and they hadn't seen it in any of their books.

"To the government?" Lester Yellow Hawk asked him back.

"No-o," said Mr. Spooner. "That is not exactly what I mean. Can someone else tell me to whom this school belongs?"

"The teachers," suggested Gloria Jean White Eagle.

"No, Gloria Jean," said Mr. Spooner. "The teachers work in the school and are very interested in it. Your teacher, Miss Hansen, left her own family and came all the way from eastern South Dakota to teach you. Mrs. Spooner and I have given most of our lives to teaching in reservation schools, but the school does not belong to us."

Alice Tomahawk decided that she knew the answer. "It belongs to us," she spoke out, "because we're the ones getting educated here."

"Correct, Alice," beamed Mr. Spooner. "You are a child who uses her head. Now can you answer another question for me? Who is most interested in having you get a good education in this school?"

"The teachers," interrupted Gloria Jean. She thought that must be the answer to something.

Alice frowned at her competitor. "Our parents," she answered. Of course, she and Frankie didn't have living parents and Grandma Tomahawk wasn't interested in the school at all, but Alice knew that was the right answer because parents and grandparents should be the ones most interested in children's education. If Grandma wasn't interested in their education, it was because something was wrong.

Mrs. Two Bears felt that Mr. Spooner wasn't coming to the point. "You go home and tell your parents to come to the meeting," she ordered the

children. "It is very important because we want to hold an election of officers. And we also want to get some volunteers to help paint the school and fix the doors. There will be notices put up in the stores so no one will have the excuse of not knowing the date or time." She glared at Gloria Jean. "And there will be food of some kind," she promised.

When Mrs. Two Bears and Mr. Spooner had left the fourth-grade room to go to the other cottage, Miss Hansen explained more about the PTA meeting to the children.

"I hope that all of your parents will come," she said, "because I want to meet them. And this is your meeting just as it is your school. We have been discussing the first PTA meeting at the teachers' cottage and we want you children to have a hand in it. Some of you will meet with Mrs. Burnt Hat in the dining room and plan the menu. Others will have kitchen and cleanup duties. All of you will be hosts and hostesses and come to introduce your parents to your teacher."

Miss Hansen took a paper from her desk and scanned it. "These pupils have been suggested for committees," she informed them.

She read off the names then wrote them on the board. Alice Tomahawk, Linda Running Wolf and Gloria Jean White Eagle were to meet with some fifth and sixth graders to plan the refreshments. There were other duties. Some children were to help set the tables in the dining room and others were to clean and decorate the community cabin for the meeting after supper.

Frankie's heart sank. He was on the dishwashing committee.

"But even more important than working on a committee is the responsibility each one of you has to see that his parents attend," Miss Hansen pointed out to them.

Alice waved her hand around her head. Miss Hansen nodded to her with a smile.

"Will your parents come, Miss Hansen," asked the little girl eagerly, "so we can meet them?"

Miss Hansen's blue eyes widened. Then they shone like bluebells sprinkled with dew, as Alice had described them in her poem.

"That is a splendid idea, Alice," she admitted. "I must confess that I hadn't even thought of it. But now I think it would be wonderful if my parents would drive here for the meeting and see my new school and my bright pupils. I will make it my responsibility to see that they come."

When Frankie and Alice arrived home,

Grandma and Little Brave were not "smoking the peace pipe" together. Grandma was angry with the raccoon. He had carried her old moccasin off and she couldn't find it. It was the one which was usually kicked around the stove legs. Although it had no mate, Grandma thought that she might need it sometime. And if she ever did, it wouldn't be underfoot because the mischievous little animal had carried it away.

But Little Brave wasn't angry with Grandma at all. He followed the moccasins that were on her feet from stove to cupboard and sat up on his hindlegs begging her to play the "five centses" game with him.

For once Alice stood up for the raccoon. "He didn't want that dirty old shoe around," she said. "He's clean." Then she went on to tell her grandmother about the PTA meeting. "I'm on the food committee," she announced proudly. "We met during afternoon recess and decided to have a supper for the parents before the meeting. We're going to have hamburgers and cakes for supper and I'm going to help Mrs. Burnt Hat make the cakes."

Mrs. Burnt Hat was the school cook. She came on the bus with her husband in the morning but walked home after lunch.

Grandma Tomahawk showed some interest. She forgot about the lost moccasin. "What kind cake?" she asked.

"Chocolate and coconut and banana," answered Alice. "And Mrs. Burnt Hat says we have to have a salad but nobody has to eat it. Won't you come, Grandma? You've never seen our school. Today teacher pinned my spelling paper on the board and it may still be there."

Frankie looked up from gently pulling Little Brave's fluffy striped tail. "Don't go, Grandma," he warned. "They're just trying to catch people for the PTA."

"White Eagles going?" asked Grandma.

"Sure they'll go," said Alice. "They like hamburgers and cakes. Gloria Jean is on the food committee too."

"Teacher Says going?" asked Grandma.

"Of course," replied Alice. "She wants to meet all our parents. And her parents are coming, too, because they want to see how their daughter is doing in school."

"Who else?" asked Grandma Tomahawk. "Who else going to big chaw?"

"Mrs. Two Bears because she's the president and—" But Alice immediately realized that she had spoken the wrong name. Mrs. Two Bears was one of the younger women who had the place on the tribal council which Grandma felt belonged to her.

Grandma Tomahawk grunted and reached for the empty oatmeal box in which she kept her coins. "PTA belong Mrs. Two Bears," she said. "Council belong Mrs. Two Bears. Me stay home."

Alice was disappointed. "The PTA may belong to Mrs. Two Bears," argued Alice, "but the school belongs to us children. It doesn't belong to the government or the teachers or anybody but us children. So our parents and grandmothers should take an interest in it."

Grandma thrust out her lower lip. "School belong Mrs. Two Bears," she sulked. "Me uncivilized old Indian. Talk bad English. Not go PTA."

96

# X

GRANDMA TOMAHAWK and Little Brave patched up their quarrel. Everything was peaceful over the weekend. They played the "five centses" game one day, and the next they played hide-and-find although Grandma didn't find her old moccasin.

Frankie thought of going into the cottonwoods to look for it but cloud shadows were moving across the prairie and thunderheads gathering in the sky.

Alice came tripping home in fine humor. "Mrs. White Eagle invited us over to watch TV this afternoon," she told Frankie. "There's going to be a western."

Frankie didn't mind daring a walk under the threatening sky to see a western. They left Grandma and Little Brave in a friendly mood, taking turns sipping the sweet pancake syrup.

It was like a movie theater in the White Eagle house. All the chairs in the room faced the TV. Mrs. White Eagle had draped her fringed summer shawl over the top of it for decoration. She was sitting in the big overstuffed chair. She had been sitting there most of that Sunday with her eyes glued to the screen. She didn't even know that there was going to be a storm.

The Tomahawk children and the little White Eagles preferred to sit on the floor and lean back against the chairs.

Mr. White Eagle came to the door with his gun in his hand. "I just came past the sorghum field and saw those antelopes there again," he told Mrs. White Eagle.

She was upset at sight of the gun. "Don't you dare shoot those antelopes on Sunday," she cried.

"I'm not going to kill them," replied Mr. White Eagle grimly, "but I'm going to scare them all the way to Nebraska."

He left and everyone silently watched the TV. A white man was talking about soil erosion. There were scenes of dust storms and deserts.

Then the man came back and urged South Dakota farmers to plant shelter belts. The scene switched to a neat row of trees between two fields of tall wheat. It was like the programs the children were shown on the TV at school.

Frankie and Abel began to wrestle on the rug. Mrs. White Eagle yawned and turned the knob of the TV. The other station had a play about some rich women at a party. Mrs. White Eagle and the girls were fascinated by their gowns and jewels, but Frankie and Abel began crawling on all fours and chasing each other around the furniture.

At last it was time for the western. Their old friend, Wagon Boss, was in new trouble. He was guiding a wagon train of pioneers across the plains. Among them was a bad man who kept doing sneaky things such as sawing the spokes of wagon wheels and running off to plot with the Indians. Wagon Boss was kept busy giving orders and keeping one eye on the bad man.

Frankie tingled at the scenes in the Indian camp. The drums were beating and the warriors dancing in their buckskins and feathers. They were preparing to attack the pioneers. The boy envied them. He hoped they would win out although that seldom happened unless the story was about General Custer.

There were louder rumbles than those of the drums on TV. The storm had broken. Outside the Thunderbird was flying over .the prairie. Lightning zigzagged from his claws and thunder rolled from his wings. As he flapped through the air, the lake of water on his back spilled over the thirsty fields and dry prairie.

"Mr. Kirk says it's dangerous to have electric things on during a thunderstorm," said Gloria Jean. "He says you shouldn't sew with a needle or cut with scissors because they draw electricity."

Mrs. White Eagle grunted. "White people are full of superstitions," she scoffed.

Besides, the picture was getting more and more exciting. The Indians attacked the wagon train but were repulsed because Wagon Boss was so smart and brave. The attackers withdrew, somewhat to Frankie's disappointment.

But the Indians had fifteen more minutes on

the program so they thought up a new plan. They were going to stampede a herd of buffalo through the circle of wagons. Frankie leaned forward tensely. This was what it would be like if the buffalo herd returned as Jim Sees Hawk had predicted. He began biting his nails like a squirrel with a nut.

Blue lightning flashed through the room. Mrs. White Eagle and the girls squealed. But no one turned off the TV. The buffalo were knocking the wagons over. They were trampling wood and canvas into the dirt. How could Wagon Boss ever save his people now?

A terrific explosion rocked the room. The glass of the TV screen shattered. Wagon Boss, the pioneers and the buffalo vanished.

Frankie felt as if he had been trampled by the buffalo. Gloria Jean and Alice were crying and screaming. They thought that Mrs. White Eagle had fainted because she didn't move.

"The lightning!" sobbed Gloria Jean hysterically. "The lightning hit us!"

Then they heard Mr. White Eagle's voice behind them. "It's just me," he assured them. "It wasn't the lightning."

They all turned. Even Mrs. White Eagle feebly turned her head. Mr. White Eagle stood in the doorway with his gun in his hands and a dazed look on his face.

"I shot the TV," he confessed. "I didn't want those white people to get hurt." Then he giggled in an embarrassed way.

Mrs. White Eagle's strength came back in a rush. She jumped from her chair and attacked him like a streak of lightning herself.

"You've broken our TV," she cried. "You've shot it all to pieces." She pointed at the glass covering the floor. "Now we don't have any TV to watch."

Mr. White Eagle had a sheepish look on his face. "It seemed so real—with the storm and everything," he apologized. "I didn't want Wagon Boss to get killed."

"He never gets killed," shouted Mrs. White Eagle.

She went to the kitchen to get a broom. She was shaking so hard with fright and anger that the children thought that she was going to use the broom on Mr. White Eagle.

"We'll buy a new TV," said Mr. White Eagle. "That wasn't the last one in town. I'll drive all the way there tomorrow to get one—if my car holds up. There's something wrong with it. It has started making those noises when I don't do anything."

Mrs. White Eagle was not satisfied. "We'll never know what happened to the wagon train," she declared. "Never, never. You and your antelopes!"

Mr. White Eagle clicked the empty cartridge from his gun. "They weren't there when I got back," he said. "They must have taken shelter in the break. So I came home."

Mrs. White Eagle was sweeping the glass into a dustpan with clinking strokes. "Why didn't you wait until the program was over?" she asked in despair.

In all the excitement no one noticed that the sun had come out radiantly and that the rainbow flowers were blooming in their arch over the prairie.

Frankie and Alice felt that it was time to leave. There was no more TV to watch and the White Eagles were busy cleaning up glass.

Frankie took his shoes off so that he could walk barefoot in the mud. He liked the soft cool feel of it sloshing between his toes. Alice took her shoes off so that she wouldn't get them muddy.

The dying prairie had been brought to life again by the Thunderbird's shower. The rabbit sage sparkled. The purple flowers of the thistles were as bright as Lily Her Many Horses' chicken. Meadowlarks flew joyously, their yellow breasts flashing. It seemed like spring instead of early fall.

Frankie and Alice took deep breaths of the freshly-washed air.

"I think today was as exciting as being a pioneer," said Alice.

When Grandma Tomahawk heard what had happened at the White Eagle house, she shook with mirth. "Charlie White Eagle heap big TV hunter," she laughed. "Shoot TV instead of antelope."

# XI

GRANDMA TOMAHAWK was on the warpath. She didn't need paint on her face and feathers in her hair to show her rage. It twisted her lips and burned her eyes.

"Raccoon got to go," she greeted Frankie when he came home one day. "No more raccoon in my house. No more raccoon on my place."

Frankie couldn't imagine what had turned her so fiercely against Little Brave.

"Why?" asked the boy in alarm. "What has he done now?"

"Him bad stealer," hissed Grandma. "Steal all my five centses. Not hide in coffeepot. Cheat."

Frankie soon satisfied himself that it was true. There were no nickels in the cabin or on the ground outside. The coffeepot was empty. There was only flour and coffee in the big cans. The money wasn't in the stove or the woodbox. The Sioux and buffalo had vanished as completely as those on the White Eagles' TV screen.

Little Brave followed the Tomahawks around as they searched in every place imaginable. He acted as if he were trying to help them. But he didn't lead them to the hideout where he had cached the nickels.

Grandma would stop from time to time to shout "stealer" at him, but he only grinned back in a friendly way.

"I knew that raccoon was going to do something real bad," said Alice. She had never forgotten what he had done to her blouse and socks.

Frankie went to the cottonwoods to look for the money. Their leaves were clenched into green fists by the wind. Their bark was rough to climb. But Frankie scaled tree after tree and pushed his arm into any holes he could find in them. He frightened a family of squirrels into squeaks and had his fingers snapped by a cross owl. He sighed hopelessly. Outdoors was so big. There were so many places that Little Brave could have put the coins.

Frankie finally gave up and walked home, his head bowed and his hands in his pockets. Grandma met him at the door.

"Take raccoon back to Jim Sees Hawk," she ordered. "Him not welcome no more."

"That's where he belongs," Alice backed Grandma. "They're both uncivilized."

Frankie tried to plead with Grandma. He would make a cage for Little Brave. He would quit school and go to work so that he could make money to pay back what had been stolen.

"No," declared Grandma, her back as straight as a prairie dog guarding its hole. "Him bad stealer." She was so indignant that she broke into Sioux. "He shall never walk in my trail again as long as the grass grows, the rivers flow and the sun sets in the west."

Frankie knew that Grandma Tomahawk meant what she had said.

"I can't take him back to Jim Sees Hawk until Saturday," he said. "He lives halfway to Oak Grove, way down the creek."

Grandma pointed sternly at Little Brave. "Him

leave tomorrow or me make raccoon robe," she threatened.

Frankie's heart felt as empty as a bird nest in the winter. He made a leash for Little Brave with a piece of rope and tied him to a post supporting the tent. He didn't know what to do with his raccoon until he had the free time to take him back to Jim Sees Hawk. But he wouldn't be an Indian taker—or whatever white men called it. He would just ask Jim to keep his pet for him. The raccoon would still belong to Frankie.

Grandma's threat to make Little Brave into a robe frightened the boy. How could he dare leave the raccoon tomorrow while he was away at school?

Then a faint hope raised his spirits. Miss Hansen had once suggested that he bring his raccoon to school so that she could see it. She had been real interested in Little Brave even though she thought his name was Spot. Perhaps she would let him keep the animal at school for a few days like Myron Two Bears had kept his rabbit.

Hai-yai, it would be a pleasure to go to school

knowing that Little Brave would be waiting for him there every day. Perhaps Miss Hansen would like the raccoon so much she would keep him all year. Frankie would never be tempted to play hookie then.

He loosened Little Brave's rope, plumped a pillow at his head for the night and snuggled the raccoon close to him. They were alone in the tent with all the mysterious spirits of the night sighing and whispering around them. Grandma slept in the cabin with Alice. She was too outraged to sleep under the same canvas with the "bad stealer."

Little Brave was restless but he waited until Frankie was fast asleep. Then he left the warmth of the carpet and crept out into the starry rustling night. He was going to play with Grandma Tomahawk's "five centses" because he knew exactly where they were.

# XII

LITTLE BRAVE was more popular with the children on the bus than with Grandma. They left their seats and crowded around him.

"You kids get back in your seats," yelled Hiram Burnt Hat. "You'll bust the springs on that side." But he was interested in Little Brave too. "So we've got a new pupil," he said to Frankie. "Is he going to be in fourth grade?"

Frankie hoped so. He explained that he wanted to keep his raccoon at school until Saturday anyway.

"Don't think he'll be in fourth grade that long," said Hiram. "Jiminy! Raccoons are mischeevious and I don't think those white teachers will like it. There's some wire fencing and a tent frame in the toolroom. I'll make a cage for him this morning while I'm down mixing paint—just in case he gets expelled from the fourth grade."

Hiram was reminded of why he was going to mix paint. "Mr. Spooner's going to start painting by himself since your lazy parents won't help him," he announced to the whole busload. "Winter'll be here in no time and then it will be too late for any outside work."

Frankie knew that was true. It had been cold in the tent last night, even though the sun had risen so brightly in the morning.

Soon the Cold Maker would ride his white horse down from the north. He would come in the first snowstorm, freezing the creeks and laying a white blanket over the cold prairie. He would frostbite children's fingers and toes and bring on Grandma's chilblains. Sometimes he would make the school bus so cold that it wouldn't start, or he would block the roads so there couldn't be any school.

Little Brave would be asleep in some snug hole then and wouldn't wake until spring. Frankie wished that the raccoon had gone to sleep for the winter earlier—before he had carried off Grandma's nickels. But Little Brave didn't act the least bit sleepy. He pulled the button off Abel White Eagle's sweater and made a girl in front scream by climbing on back of her seat and trying to stick his nose in her ear.

Miss Hansen was as interested in the raccoon as the children and Hiram. "Spot is so bright-eyed," she said. "I think he must be the most intelligent of his species."

"He's real smart hiding things where people can't find them," admitted Frankie.

"Then we will have to watch our books and pencils," warned the teacher.

Frankie got down to business. "Can he stay here, Miss Hansen?" he pleaded. "He's real clean. He washes things all the time."

"We shall see how it works out," answered his teacher cautiously. "Perhaps Spot can give the class a lesson in cleanliness right now."

The children enjoyed Little Brave's lesson. Miss Hansen ran some water in the basin and the raccoon paddled in it with his forepaws.

"Even a little wild animal is interested in cleanliness," Miss Hansen pointed out to the class. "We should wash our hands often too."

One of the children handed the raccoon an apple from his pocket and Little Brave sloshed it through the water before he ate it.

"This is a lesson for us," said Miss Hansen. "We should never eat a piece of fruit or a raw vegetable without washing it thoroughly."

Little Brave looked at her sharply and waited to give another lesson. A girl passed her head scarf to the raccoon and he spent quite some time pulling and kneading it in the washbasin.

"Spot will be our model," said the teacher. "We must always keep our clothing clean. Each group of you children draw and color a poster about cleanliness. And make the picture of a raccoon on it. All of you have seen the posters of the bear with the warnings about the danger of fire. Make a poster with Spotty the Raccoon urging everyone to have clean hands and clean clothing and to eat clean food."

Frankie thought that it was time to correct Miss Hansen if his raccoon's name was going to be on the posters.

"His name is Little Brave," he told Miss Hansen.

"I thought you said that it was Spot," she reminded him.

"Spot's my brother's horse," put in Gloria Jean. "He doesn't like water except to drink it."

"His name is Little Brave now," said Frankie without further explanation. Miss Hansen hadn't given him a satisfactory answer to the length of time the raccoon could stay at the school. "May he stay here in the fourth grade today?" asked Frankie. "Hiram said he'd make a cage and keep him in the toolroom. But Little Brave likes to be with people."

"I suppose that he can visit for the day and go into Hiram's cage when school is over," said the teacher. "We'll see how it works out anyway," she repeated.

It worked out only long enough for the children to use Little Brave as a model for their posters. After that they couldn't keep their minds on their lessons and the raccoon couldn't keep his paws out of anything. He dug into the trash can and wanted to look in everybody's desk shelf. The children were in gales of giggles.

"Frank, take Spot to Hiram," ordered Miss

Hansen. "I mean take Little Brave to Hiram."

Frankie was sorry that Little Brave had been expelled so soon. He carried the raccoon out the door and down the steps. The toolroom was the basement of the community cabin. The weed mower, gardening and carpentry tools and other work implements were stored there. It was large and well-lighted because it was built on the side of a hill.

Hiram Burnt Hat was in the room putting the finishing touches on the cage. "This wire is strong enough to hold a bear," he said. "Just leave the little fellow loose and close the door good behind you. I'll put him in jail before I leave."

Frankie left Little Brave examining the wire. The boy went back to his classroom. He would save some of his lunch to take to his pet, especially if there were cookies for dessert. Miss Hansen hadn't told him how long he could keep Little Brave in the toolroom, but Myron Two Bears had left his pet rabbit in the cottage for three days and two pigs had lived behind the bus shed until they were full grown.

After school Frankie held up the bus by running down to the toolroom to tell Little Brave good-by. The raccoon was in jail with the door latched on the outside. He was very unhappy because he had just found out that he was inside the wire instead of outside.

Frankie reached his fingers through the cage and the raccoon clung to them and cried like a child being left behind by its mother. When Frankie turned to go, Little Brave stood on his hind legs and pushed his nose and paws through the wire as far as they would go. He cried louder.

The boy was as unhappy as his pet. He came back and rubbed Little Brave's nose. Then he quickly unlatched the cage door and ran out without looking back. He closed the toolroom door securely behind him.

Frankie went home to a cabin that seemed dreary and empty without a mischievous little raccoon playing around it.

Grandma Tomahawk was making a rice pudding. Since she had no coins with which to play the Indian and buffalo game, she had decided to cook up some of the rice in the cupboard to get rid of it. She put a lot of sugar in the rice and found out that it improved the taste.

Frankie and Alice liked the rice pudding.

"Why didn't you make any before?" asked Alice. "See how good the food is when you take time to cook it right."

Frankie wished Little Brave were there to eat the pudding because he loved sweet things. He hoped that the raccoon had discovered that the cage door was unlatched so he could play around in the toolroom during the night. Frankie couldn't think of any mischief he could do there. There were no nickels or freshly-washed clothes. And he wouldn't be able to carry anything away into the woods.

# XIII

FRANKIE wanted to run down to see Little Brave when he reached school next morning. But the bus was late and the teachers were impatient to begin classes. The boy didn't want to do anything that would cause trouble with his teacher and make her change her mind about keeping Little Brave.

Lessons went smoothly. Miss Hansen had the children vote for the best cleanliness poster then tacked the winning one on the bulletin board. Frankie thought that it was an excellent likeness of his raccoon.

Writing in the work books went along quietly until the children heard a commotion in Mrs. Spooner's room next door. There was a shuffling of feet and the door between the rooms was flung open. Mrs. Spooner entered followed by Hiram Burnt Hat.

"Is Frank Tomahawk present?" demanded Mrs. Spooner in her most severe voice. Frankie was startled. He wondered what he had done wrong. He was trying so hard to be a good student—until Saturday anyway.

Mrs. Spooner's eyes found him. "Frank Tomahawk," she said. "Take your raccoon off the school property immediately."

Hiram rolled his eyes around. "He's made an awful mess in the toolroom," he explained to Miss Hansen. "Paint all over the place and the tools ruined. I don't see for the life of me how he ever got out. I hooked that latch myself."

Frankie was horrified. Paint! Hiram had said something about mixing paint for Mr. Spooner.

"Oh, I'm to blame," said Miss Hansen hastily. "I told Frank that he could keep his raccoon here for a while. I've been encouraging the children to bring their pets to school."

"No more pets," declared Mrs. Spooner. "The toolroom is in a shambles according to Hiram. Everything seems to happen when my husband is away at the Agency."

Frankie tried to think. "I'm going to take Little Brave to Jim Sees Hawk Saturday," he told Mrs.

Spooner. "Grandma won't let me keep him at home."

"Take the raccoon out somewhere and turn it loose," Mrs. Spooner ordered Frank. "Wild animals weren't meant to be pets. Set it loose and let it go wild. That is the best thing."

Hiram Burnt Hat tried to explain to Frankie. "He's ruined a gallon of paint and my tools too," he said. "I can't understand it. I'd of sworn that cage would hold a bear."

Frankie understood it and he was desolate. Turn his raccoon loose! Everyone and everything was against him. He rose slowly. "I'll take Little Brave away," he said in a low voice.

Mrs. Spooner repeated her order to Miss Hansen. "No more pets," she laid down the law.

Hiram wanted to have the last word with the teachers so that they would respect him. "Jiminy!" he exclaimed. "I sure got a mess to clean up."

Frankie followed him out of the room. He heard footsteps behind him on the steps. A hand was laid on his shoulder. It was Miss Hansen.

"I know how you feel, Frank," she said gently.

"I had to give up my little banty rooster too. But a tractor ran over him."

Frankie walked faster to get away from Miss Hansen but she doggedly kept up with him. "In the old days," she said, "Indian boys showed their courage by bearing self-inflicted pain. Nowadays the pain is all inside and calls for even more bravery."

The boy shook loose from her touch and hurried to catch up with Hiram.

Dramatically the man opened the door to the toolroom and pointed out the bucket of white paint that he had mixed before going home the night before.

"I covered it with a board too," said Hiram. "And that coon was sitting in his cage watching me just as nice as you please. I don't see how he unlatched that door."

Frankie knew, but it was too late. Hiram hadn't exaggerated. Little Brave had pushed the board off the bucket. He had gathered nails, screwdrivers, hammers and everything he could lay his paws on. He had carried them to the bucket and dropped them into the white paint. Then he had played in it himself. There were trails of little white tracks all over the cement floor. Little Brave had spent the night in "busy work," as the teacher might have called it.

Now he sat satisfied in the cage with the door open. His paws and nose were white. There

were blotches of white on his fur. He looked as if the Cold Maker had caught him.

"Jiminy!" exclaimed Hiram. "He's as big a mess as this room."

Little Brave came out of the cage to meet Frankie. The boy silently lifted him into his arms.

His eyes were filling with tears but he tried to blink them back. He didn't want Hiram to see a Sioux boy cry.

He hurried out of the schoolyard to the road. He wasn't going to set his raccoon loose. He was going to run away. He was going to live like an old-time Indian and never have anything to do with school or white people again. He wouldn't tell anyone but Jim Sees Hawk. He would go to him to find out how he could survive out on the prairie during the winter.

Frankie stamped some dead sunflowers and the wind carried the piney smell of the crushed seeds to his nose. He slid under a wire fence and stepped into the pathless prairie. From now on his life would be without paths to follow.

He put Little Brave down and the raccoon dogged his heels. Ahead of him were hills pricked with pines, like warbonnets gathered in council. The wind was in his face. It made him feel free. The brown prairie and low hills belonged to him in the same way as they belonged to the brown hawk battling the wind over the sumacs.

If he cut through the hills, he would reach the

creek sooner. He turned past gray cutbanks and followed a rough break. He walked with his head down to watch his footing.

When he raised his head, he saw the buffalo. Frankie stopped in his tracks. Little Brave stopped too. The great buffalo was coming out of the hills. And behind it, as far as Frankie's eyes could see, were moving bodies. The buffalo herd was coming back! Jim Sees Hawk had been right after all.

Frankie was filled with exultation. At the time when he needed them most, the buffalo were coming back to drive the white people away and restore the prairie to the Indians. He scrambled out of the break, calling Little Brave to keep up with him. He must go straight to Jim Sees Hawk with the wonderful news.

Then a terrible scene flashed through his mind. He remembered the TV show. He could see the buffalo turning the wagons over. He could see the terrified faces of the pioneers. That was going to happen to his school. Jim Sees Hawk had said so.

Frankie stopped again. The wind tore at him

with fresh fury, trying to pull him on to Jim Sees Hawk. He fought the wind and himself.

The school belonged to him. It belonged to every Indian child. It would be a shame if their beautiful yellow desks were crushed. The children would be hurt, too, and Miss Hansen.

Teacher had been kind to him many times but he hadn't even realized it until now. She had left her own family to come to the reservation to teach Sioux children. She had even understood how he felt about losing Little Brave.

He saw that the great buffalo was headed toward the school as it came past the outcroppings of rock. And the dark moving creatures on the hill were going the same way. He couldn't see them distinctly but they looked like the herd on the TV show.

Frankie was panic-stricken. He must get back to the school before the buffalo got there. He must warn the teachers and children. Perhaps they could barricade all the doors and withstand the buffalo siege.

He ran so fast that his lungs and legs felt as if they were shot full of arrows. His legs grew numb but he forced them to go on. He ran like the whitetail deer.

Frankie burst into the fourth-grade room with wild eyes. "The buffalo herd!" he panted. "It's come back. It's going to knock the school over."

Miss Hansen was alarmed but not by the news of the buffalo herd. She thought that Frankie's grief at parting with his raccoon had hurt his mind. She tried to be calm although all of the children were running to the window.

"Sit down, Frank," she said soothingly. "You're all out of breath and you've had a difficult day. Sit down at your desk until you catch your breath."

But Frankie thought that would be wasting precious time. "I saw the buffalo coming here," he continued breathlessly. "The hills were full of them."

"I don't see anything but Mr. White Eagle's car going down the road," said Myrna Flying Hawk. Perhaps Frankie thought that it was a buffalo. It was making awfully queer noises.

Gloria Jean had her own explanation. "It's the TV we saw last Sunday," she told Miss Hansen. "Even Papa thought the buffalo were real."

Frankie dropped his head into his arms hopelessly. No one believed that he had seen the buffalo. They wouldn't do anything about it.

"Come back to your seats, children," said Miss Hansen. "After Frankie has rested, he can tell us about the buffalo on the TV show."

Another sharp arrow of alarm pierced Frankie. He had forgotten all about Little Brave. He had deserted him on the prairie. But the raccoon couldn't be far behind. He had surely followed Frankie.

He tried again when his breath was back in his body. "I really did see a buffalo, Miss Hansen," he argued. "A whole herd of them. And they're coming this way."

Miss Hansen breathed a little easier. Frankie seemed more normal now. Perhaps this was some trick to keep his raccoon. But the children ran to the windows again at his words.

Their teacher spoke to them sharply. They returned to their seats a second time but there was no more studying. No one could keep his mind on books.

Miss Hansen was out of patience. She had done everything that she could to win over this strange boy and to try to understand him. It had been useless. He would always be a problem child.

She closed the geography book with a snap. "Frank Tomahawk," she said sternly, "you have disrupted the whole routine for the day. Now I want you to stand up and tell this class that you made up the story about the buffalo."

Frankie stubbornly shook his head. Miss Hansen rose from her desk. "Come with me, Frank," she said. "I am going to take you next door to have a little talk with Mrs. Spooner since Mr. Spooner is away on business."

Frank obeyed. Perhaps Mrs. Spooner would believe him and do something to protect the school. But when Miss Hansen left him standing by Mrs. Spooner's desk and he looked at her set face, he knew that the hope was vain.

"So you say that you saw a buffalo on the prairie, Frank," she said with a thin, chilly smile. "That is nonsense. You know that there are no longer any wild bison in this country. There are only the herds in the national parks and on private ranches. There haven't been any wild herds around here for many years—certainly before your time."

"They've come back," said Frankie. "Jim Sees Hawk said they would."

Mrs. Spooner grew impatient. She wasn't used to having children argue with her. She raised her hand and looked at her wrist watch. "Frank Tomahawk," she said in a wintry voice, "I will give you five minutes to tell me that you didn't see a buffalo."

The minutes ticked away on the wall clock too. Frankie's back sagged but his lips were set in a straight line. Mrs. Spooner raised her eyes from her watch and glanced idly out of the window. Her face set like a mask and her eyes were popped. "Good heavens!" she cried. "There is a buffalo on the playground!"

# XIV

AS SOON AS she saw the buffalo on the playground, Mrs. Spooner sprang into action.

"Don't leave this room," she commanded the children. "Even strange cows can be dangerous. Abel White Eagle, you will see that my order is obeyed."

She hurried to Miss Hansen's room with Frankie. "Frank told the truth," she admitted to the fourth-grade teacher. "There is a buffalo on the schoolgrounds. Keep the children in while I warn Miss Waring's cottage and find Hiram to drive it away. And please keep an eye on my children too. Close the windows and keep the outer doors closed."

The children were disappointed when the windows were pulled down but they hung over the draft boards and looked through the glass.

They could see the buffalo. It looked like a great bull with a brown shag rug thrown over its head and shoulders. It was standing by the slide, looking over the playground as if it were considering it for a pasture.

Most of the children had never seen a real buffalo before. They were astonished at its size and shape.

"Here comes Hiram with a shovel," cried Amos White Deer.

They watched him advance to the shaggy beast. He brandished the shovel.

"Git!" he shouted. "Go 'way! Scat!"

The buffalo looked at him with mean little eyes. It pawed the ground. Hiram retreated a few steps. The buffalo snorted. It raised its tail and lowered its head. It charged the man.

Hiram dropped the shovel and ran. The nearest refuge was the windmill. He streaked up its frame like a frightened squirrel. From a safe perch, he yelled at the buffalo.

"Go home, you overgrown cow," he shouted. "Git!"

The buffalo butted the windmill. Inside the

schoolhouse, the children were pressing each other against the windows. There had never been such excitement at the Little Axe school.

Mrs. Spooner returned to the cottage. "Everyone stay inside," she repeated her order to the fourth grade. "The beast is definitely vicious. I will make a run for the house and call the Agency for help."

Frankie felt a sudden admiration for Mrs. Spooner. She was stern but she was brave and cool-headed too. She was like Wagon Boss, trying to protect the people in her care.

Frankie was at one of the windows. Miss Hansen tried to get the children back to their seats but it was impossible.

"If my father was here, he would shoot that buffalo," boasted Gloria Jean White Eagle.

Then they saw a frightening sight. Alice Tomahawk was coming toward the playground from the road. She was walking with her head low in the wind and her feet dragging dispiritedly. She would walk right near the buffalo.

Miss Hansen put her fingers to her cheeks. "Oh, my goodness," she cried. "Alice Tomahawk! I sent her to find you, Frank, because it took so long for you to come back."

As she spoke, she rapped against the window glass with all her strength to catch Alice's attention. The little girl looked up. Thinking that teacher was signaling her to hurry, Alice walked faster across the playground.

Frankie hadn't even noticed that his sister was absent. So much had been happening to him. It was his fault that she was out on the playground with the dangerous buffalo.

His bow and arrows were still in the display. If only Abel had sharpened the arrows. He didn't tell anyone what he was going to do. He hurried to the shelf and pulled the bow off the nail and snatched two arrows. As Miss Hansen strained to raise a window, Frankie raced to the door and ran out.

The buffalo had seen Alice. It was going toward her now with its head lowered. Alice saw the great beast and froze like a small bird awaiting the swoop of a hawk.

But Frankie was coming to her rescue. His arrow was braced against the bowstring. He ran close to the buffalo so that the arrow would strike with more force.

Nothing had ever looked bigger to the boy than that buffalo. Its massive hump rose up like a mountain. Its woolly head was three or four times as large as a bull's. Its strong horns curved upward.

Frankie tried to keep his hand from trembling as he pulled the arrow back. It swished through the air and struck the beast on the shoulder, then fell to the ground. The buffalo looked at his small adversary with more surprise than anger. Frankie let the other arrow fly. It didn't even hit its mark, but the great beast studied Frankie with a bewildered expression in its little bloodshot eyes. Then it slowly turned on its four hoofs and jogged away. It must have thought that the old-time Indian hunters were coming back.

Alice had already gained safety in the cottage. Hiram Burnt Hat began descending the windmill. Frankie felt foolish because he hadn't killed the buffalo. He hadn't even hit it the second time. But he was glad that his unexpected attack had scared the beast away.

Before he went back to the cottage, his eyes swept the crimped horizon to see if the rest of the herd was coming. But there was no moving object in sight other than the lone buffalo slowly walking down the road, switching its tail and shaking its head.

Miss Hansen scarcely had time to congratulate Frankie for driving the buffalo away before Mrs. Spooner returned again.

"They told me at the Agency that it is an old buffalo that was cast out of the herd because it lost its battles with the young bulls," explained Mrs. Spooner. "It has wandered all this way from the Black Hills. Charlie Big Elk had already called them because he saw it in the pine hills with his herd of cattle. They're sending some rangers with a truck to take it back."

So those were the moving forms Frankie had seen among the hills—Charlie Big Elk's cattle. There had been only one buffalo.

The children were curious about what would happen to the old buffalo when it was brought back to the herd. Would the young bulls turn on it again?

"No, indeedy, they wouldn't dare," said Hiram Burnt Hat. "Not after it tells them its adventures on the reservation and how it was attacked by an Indian warrior and lived to tell the story."

"And how it chased another warrior up a windmill," said Mrs. Spooner shortly. "Get back to work, Hiram."

Yes, Mrs. Spooner was like Wagon Boss. She could even joke when the danger was over.

Frankie hoped that he would be worthy to take her orders when he reached the fifth grade.

Miss Hansen apologized to Frankie in front of the whole class. "You were in the right, Frank," she admitted. "You really did see a buffalo."

Frankie flushed and felt ill at ease. "I wasn't all right," he admitted manfully. "I was running away from school."

Miss Hansen was amazed at this news. "But you came back," she reminded him.

"I didn't want the buffalo to knock the school down," said Frankie. "I thought there was a whole herd of them." He grinned sheepishly because he had taken Charlie Big Elk's cattle for buffalo.

"Why didn't you want the school to be damaged?" Miss Hansen followed up.

Frankie wished that she would stop asking him questions. But he didn't feel sullen about answering them. He only felt embarrassed because all of the children were listening.

"Because it's our school," he finally admitted. "Because I wish I'd studied last year and gone on with my own class."

Miss Hansen didn't ask him any more questions. But when the class was dismissed at the end of the day, she called him to her desk for a private talk.

"Would you be willing to do some extra studying so that you could catch up with your class and go into the fifth grade by Christmas?" she asked him.

Frankie shifted his weight from one foot to the other. He ran his fingers through his scalplock. "Alice might help me," he said. And she better not be too bossy about it because he had saved her from the buffalo.

"*I* would help you," said Miss Hansen. "If you

are willing to stay in during recesses, I will coach you."

Frankie nodded as if it wasn't too important and he would be doing her a favor. His gratitude was so great that he was too shy to show it. "Sure," he agreed casually.

"Then we begin tomorrow," said Miss Hansen. She handed him a reading book. "And you might spend a little time on this when you get home tonight."

Frankie thought that it had been a wonderful day. It had been full of excitement and success. If only Little Brave would come back. Perhaps the raccoon had gone to the Tomahawk cabin since that had really been its home.

Hiram Burnt Hat did not think that it had been such a wonderful day.

"Jiminy!" he exclaimed as the bus bounced over the back roads. "I hate to see my cows to-night. I've had my fill of animals for one day."

# XV

FRANKIE'S DAYS were full now that he was working hard to catch up with his own grade. It wasn't easy. Even though he studied whenever possible, one couldn't know everything like a magpie.

One thing he knew well. If he finished school he wasn't going to be a truck driver or a dust farmer. With a good education he could be on the tribal council, a leader among his people. The road ahead was still hidden in mist though.

He couldn't get over his longing for Little Brave. Why hadn't the raccoon come back? Perhaps he had even started back that day that Frankie had seen the buffalo. Perhaps somewhere along the trail he had met a Jim Sees Hawk raccoon who had persuaded him to desert humans. It might have been only a sniff at some bush or stone. Or something the wind had whispered into his furry ears.

The boy went to see Jim Sees Hawk one Saturday to find out if Little Brave might have gone back to him.

He had felt so close to Jim before, but now a difference lay between them. It must have been caused by Frankie's decision to follow the white man's path. Anyway, nothing was the same.

"How?" asked the old man. And it was as if he asked, "How did this happen? How did you change so much in a moon?"

Frankie knew that he had changed. Jim Sees Hawk looked different too. He looked like a poor, uncivilized old Indian who had outlived his own kind. His tent on the creek looked dreary and lonely.

"The raccoon did not come back," said Jim. "I gave him to you." Frankie felt reproach in his voice. Although Jim Sees Hawk was dirty and uncivilized, there was a dignity in his manner and words. "You have changed," said Jim. "You still have the same body but your soul has changed."

So Jim felt the same way about him. They squatted together on the ground in front of Jim's tent, but it was as if the creek flowed between them.

Frankie could not tell him about the outcast buffalo that had wandered from the Black Hills and changed his mind about school and the white people. But again the old Sioux guessed what was in the boy's mind.

"The buffalo herd will never return now," he said sadly. "I no longer hear the thunder of the hoofs."

"Yes, I know," said Frankie.

He realized that the old man had made up the story about the buffalo herd's return to comfort a discontented boy.

Frankie stayed long enough to make a polite visit. He tried not to appear eager as he hopped back on his feet.

"Good-by," he said. "I guess Little Brave went back with the wild raccoons."

"Farewell, grandson," said Jim Sees Hawk affectionately, "may the good spirits walk with you on the road ahead."

Jim spoke as if Frankie were going on some long journey from which he would never return.

It was late when Frankie reached home but the day sun had not shot all his arrows yet.

Some new trouble shadowed the Tomahawk cabin with its dark wing. Alice's eyes were red from weeping. But Grandma looked as happy as a rabbit in May.

"Iron Shells come by here," she announced. "They take you and Alice Nebraska to pick potatoes."

Alice burst into fresh tears. "I don't want to go pick potatoes in Nebraska," she howled. "I'll miss out on school. I don't want to be an old potato picker all my life. I want to go to college like teacher and get educated."

Frankie agreed with her. "We can't leave school to go potato picking," he said. "The Iron Shells will be gone for weeks. I'd miss out on my lessons with Miss Hansen. I wouldn't be able to make my grade."

Grandma crossed her hands over her breast and stared at him. "You say you work for make money raccoon stoled," she reminded him. "You pick potatoes and get five centses back for me."

The boy felt caught in his own trap. He remembered that he had offered to leave school and work to pay Grandma back the money that Little Brave had taken.

"But I've changed my mind," he told Grandma. "I want to get educated too."

"Only a rabbit caught in a snare changes its mind so fast," snapped Grandma Tomahawk in Sioux.

The children could see that it was no use to argue with their grandmother. Perhaps there was some other way to change her mind.

Then one day Frankie thought that their problem had been solved.

Little Brave came back. The boy saw him sitting on top of the squaw cooler. Its leaves were dead now and the family didn't use it much because the days were growing chilly. The Thunderbird had flown south with the other birds, not to return until spring.

Frankie thrilled at the sight of his pet sitting

144

among the brown leaves. Perhaps he was making a nest on top of the squaw cooler for his long winter sleep.

The boy noticed that the raccoon's fur was still blotched with paint but the white on his paws had turned a pinkish gray from the prairie dust. Paint couldn't be washed off. It would have to wear away. There was no doubt that it was Little Brave, but he acted strangely. He wouldn't come down to Frankie.

The boy tried to coax the raccoon with some of Grandma's pancake syrup, but there was a wildness about the animal now. It didn't seem to trust humans.

Frankie was so disappointed and hurt that he grew angry with Little Brave. He tried to shake him down but the raccoon clung to the dead branches. Frankie shook harder. The dry leaves fell in an autumn shower on the ground. Something else fell down. A handful of coins pattered over his shoulders. An old moccasin thumped to the ground.

Grandma's "five centses!" Little Brave had

hidden them on top of the squaw cooler. He had carried Grandma's moccasin up there first so it would make a pocket for the coins.

"Grandma!" shouted Frankie. "Grandma!"

He scraped the coins into his hands. As he

searched for others, Little Brave climbed down from the squaw cooler. He ran several feet away then stopped and watched Frankie with masked eyes.

"Come here, Little Brave," coaxed Frankie.

He went after the raccoon but it ran away

from him. It stopped furtively at the end of the path that led to the cottonwoods. Then Frankie knew that Little Brave had gone wild. He thought it was the last time he would ever see the raccoon.

He closed his eyes tightly to fix in his mind the way Little Brave looked with his saucy nose and black mask. When he opened them, the raccoon was gone.

"Grandma!" cried Frankie again. "I've found your money. We won't have to go pick potatoes in Nebraska."

But Grandma was not too happy. There was only a handful of coins. Frankie climbed on top of the cooler to search for the others. But Little Brave must have taken them away already. He must have been coming back to the cabin many times during the nights, patiently carrying the coins to a hollow in some tree. He would spend the winter sleeping with them—the richest raccoon in South Dakota.

"Me got full oatmeal box before," complained Grandma. "That bad stealer stoled most my five centses." She grabbed her money and clutched her moccasin to her breast. "You and Alice make potato money," she insisted.

Alice wiped her eyes and half-sobbed. "Money isn't everything," she said. "It's more important to get educated. That's what teacher says. How can Frankie and me get educated in a potato field?"

She and her brother agreed upon one thing. If they could get Grandma Tomahawk to the PTA supper at school, she might learn how important it was for children to go to school.

Miss Anna Hansen told the children that they were to write invitations to take home to their parents. She wrote a form on the green board.

*"Dear Mother and Father,"* she wrote:

*"We are going to have a PTA supper at school next Thursday night at six o'clock. We invite you to come. We want you.*

*Your son (or daughter),*
*Name"*

The children were given pieces of snow-white

paper for the invitations. They were told to use their best penmanship.

Frankie ruined two pieces of the paper before he was able to write all the way through without a mistake. "Dear Grandma," he began. As he wrote the third copy, a sudden inspiration came to him. He didn't sign the note "Frankie." He boldly signed it, "Miss Anna Hansen, fourth-grade teacher."

If Grandma Tomahawk thought that teacher had written the invitation herself, she might come. She might feel that she had to come.

When he told Alice what he had done, she was surprised that she hadn't thought of it herself. She tore up her own invitation.

"You're getting real smart," she complimented him. "I bet you'll be somebody famous some-day."

She was disappointed because she hadn't thought of it.

As the children expected, Grandma Tomahawk was very impressed with the invitation signed "Miss Anna Hansen, fourth-grade teacher."

"Teacher Says write everybody parents?" she asked.

Frankie shook his head. "No, indeed," he said. "You're the only one with an invitation to the PTA signed Miss Anna Hansen."

That was the truth anyway.

"Why Teacher Says send invite only me?" asked Grandma suspiciously. Her eyes had read and reread the piece of paper. Even if Grandma couldn't speak good English, she could read it.

Frankie wasn't smart enough to think of an explanation for that but Alice did. "It's because her parents are coming too," said the girl. "They're probably old so she wants you to be their hostess. That means you're to talk to them all evening and make them welcome."

"Me welcome Teacher Says parents?" asked Grandma in awe. "Not Pauline Two Bears?"

"Mrs. Two Bears isn't old enough," said Alice.

Grandma read the invitation over and over. No white person had ever invited her to anything on a piece of white paper.

"Teacher Says not write good," said Grandma critically. "Look like bird tracks."

Frankie flushed. He should have let Alice write the invitation because she had such a neat hand. "But she real polite," admitted the old woman. "Call me grandma." It was lucky for Frankie that "grandma" was a title of respect given by the Sioux to old women.

Grandma carried the paper inside. She tacked it to the wall next to a newspaper picture of an Indian tribal dance.

"Me go PTA supper," she announced.

Frankie and Alice were overjoyed but Alice's happiness did not last long.

"Me wear Indian dress to PTA," said Grandma. "Fancy dress me weared to Black Hills pageant."

Alice was horrified. "You can't wear Indian clothes to the supper," she cried. "The PTA is real civilized. Nobody wears Indian clothes."

But Grandma's mind was made up. "White people at pageant like my Indian clothes. Teacher Says parents white."

"*They* won't be in Indian clothes," insisted Alice. "Nobody'll be in uncivilized clothes but you. Everybody will think our grandmother looks like an old Indian."

Frankie didn't see why Alice was so upset about what Grandma wore. The important thing was to get her there. "Grandma can look like an old Indian if she wants," he defended. "And Mrs. Two Bears looks like an Indian no matter what she wears."

But Alice thought that Grandma's appearance at the PTA supper in doeskin, quills and beads would disgrace the Tomahawk family.

She even told Miss Hansen about it privately, shame reddening her face. "My grandmother's going to wear her Indian clothes to the supper," said Alice when she was able to catch Miss Hansen alone. "No matter what I say, she's still going to wear all those beads and feathers."

Miss Hansen didn't look shocked at all. "Then your grandmother is coming," she exclaimed. "Isn't that wonderful? She has never visited the school before, has she?"

Alice hung her head. "Everybody will laugh at her," said the child desperately. "I'll be passing around the hamburgers at the supper and I'll hear everybody laughing at my grandmother."

Miss Hansen looked at her intently. "Oh, I'm sure that won't happen," she said. She patted Alice's shoulder. "I promise you that I won't let it happen," she stated.

Alice didn't see how teacher could keep the PTA from laughing at Grandma Tomahawk but she knew that Miss Hansen wouldn't laugh anyway. She wanted to tell her about the potato-picking problem, but she couldn't. Potato picking in Nebraska was an even more painful subject than Indian clothes at a PTA meeting. Let Grandma tell her.

# XVI

THE TOMAHAWKS were ready for the PTA supper. Alice had washed her extra blouse and socks. She had shined her old rundown shoes and had sponged her worn serge skirt from the mission box. Her black hair hung in waves because she had put it up in rags again. On one side it made a curl.

Frankie was clean too. His hair was wet and shining from all the water and brushing. It almost lay flat on his head.

But Grandma Tomahawk made the most striking picture. Her white doeskin dress, embroidered with beads, hung in long fringes. An apron of dyed quills covered it from the breast to the knees. Her braids were lengthened by yellow eagle feathers hung on the ends. Alice shuddered every time she looked at her.

When the White Eagles came banging up to the cabin, even Mrs. White Eagle couldn't help exclaiming at Grandma's appearance.

"I bet you could get on TV," she said, and that was the best compliment Mrs. White Eagle could give anyone.

Grandma settled herself stiffly in the back seat. She didn't trust automobiles. She was sure that someday Mr. White Eagle's car was going to explode, but she was brave.

Other automobiles and trucks were driving the roads toward the school. Some families who didn't live too far away were on foot.

Soon they could see the Little Axe school through the cloud of dust. When they arrived, everyone was going to the large community log cabin. The White Eagles and the Tomahawks followed the crowd.

The cabin had inherited the old discarded school furniture. There were crooked benches and broken desks along the wall. All were occupied, and some men and children were sitting on the floor.

Mr. and Mrs. Spooner and the two teachers

were standing near the door to greet the arrivals. Mrs. Two Bears in a new blue silk dress which covered her like a tepee stood with them.

Alice made the introductions because Frankie suddenly became tongue-tied with shyness.

"This is my grandmother I told you about," she said to Miss Hansen.

Miss Hansen greeted Grandma Tomahawk warmly. "It was wonderful of you to come," she beamed. "You have made your grandchildren so happy."

Grandma smiled graciously and shook hands. Then she looked all around. "Your papa and mama," she asked. "Where?"

"They haven't arrived yet," said Miss Hansen. "They have such a long drive. But I'm sure they will be here soon."

A young woman got up from a bench to make a seat for Grandma Tomahawk. Grandma sat down majestically between Mrs. Tall Cow and Mrs. Her Many Horses. Lily was clinging to her mother's skirt. There were little bells tied into the laces of the child's shoes and they tinkled when she kicked her feet.

The two mothers turned toward Grandma and looked her up and down.

"Are you going to dance, Grandma?" asked Mrs. Her Many Horses.

"No," said Grandma Tomahawk.

"Going to sing?" asked Mrs. Tall Cow.

"No," said Grandma. "Going to chaw."

The women continued their conversation across Grandma Tomahawk's quills. Mrs. Tall Cow thought that it was shocking the way the young girls were dressing in warriors' costumes for the dances and Mrs. Her Many Horses agreed with her.

Alice hung around long enough to satisfy herself that nobody was going to laugh at her grandmother. Then she went to the dining cottage to help make the hamburgers.

Frankie had made up his mind to stay as far away from that cottage as possible. He squatted on the floor with some of the men.

He was there when Miss Hansen's parents arrived. There were excited voices at the door. Miss Hansen went outside to meet them. She proudly led her parents into the cabin.

A stunned silence fell over the assembly. Miss Hansen's parents didn't look civilized. They weren't even dressed like white people. The mother wore a black velvet dress with a bright red vest. A long white apron with inserts of crocheted lace was tied around her waist. A bib of

heavy silver ornaments hung across her breast and a starched white linen bonnet stood out in wings over her ears.

Mr. Hansen was in black knee pants with a red vest decorated with bright silver buttons.

"These are my parents," Miss Hansen announced proudly. "Mr. and Mrs. Olaf Hansen."

Surprise couldn't make Grandma Tomahawk forget why she was there. She rose quickly and went over to be hostess to teacher's parents. Mrs. Two Bears had moved toward them, but Grandma pushed herself right in front of the PTA president.

"This is Mrs. Tomahawk," Miss Hansen told her parents. "She is the grandmother of two of my best pupils."

"How!" greeted Grandma, politely putting out her hand.

"Pleased to meet you," said Mrs. Hansen, taking the thin, gnarled hand in a warm grip. Mr. Hansen shook hands as if he were pumping water from a well.

"I heard that you were wearing your beautiful Indian costume tonight," said Miss Hansen to Grandma, "so I asked my parents to wear their Norwegian dress. They didn't come to this country until after they were married, you know."

Mrs. Hansen nodded her swan-like bonnet. "Ya! Ve come from the old country," she said.

"There are many Norwegian-Americans in my home town," explained Miss Hansen. "Once a year they have a big festival and wear their native clothes."

"Ya," put in Mr. Hansen. "Have a big vedding and dance polkas. Ve are Americans now but it is good to remember the past."

Grandma was too much of an Indian to show her surprise at the Hansens. The parents of Teacher Says had even broken their English. But she couldn't hide her curiosity about Mrs. Hansen's clothes. She lifted the apron and looked at the crocheted lace. She fondled the silver ornaments.

"Real?" she asked.

"Ya," said Mrs. Hansen. "I vore them at my vedding and my mother vore them at her vedding. Old family silver. All the vay from Hardanger."

Grandma patted her own breast. "My mother wore," she said. "Real quills. Real eagle feathers. Real doeskin."

"Yee whizz," said Mr. Hansen with admiration. "Real old-time Indian duds."

Frankie was drinking in everything with his eyes and ears. He wished that Alice could be there. But she was present. Curiosity had drawn her away from the hamburgers. She stood in the doorway with her eyes as big as sunflower centers.

Miss Hansen took her parents around the room to meet everyone and Grandma Tomahawk followed. She was not going to let the Hansens be separated from her for a minute. Every time Mrs. Two Bears would try to talk to the visitors, Grandma would step in front of her and interrupt. Pauline Two Bears hadn't been invited to be their hostess.

The supper bell clanged impatiently from the dining cottage. All of the Indians swarmed toward it. Grandma Tomahawk lingered behind with the Hansens and so did Mrs. Two Bears.

Mr. Hansen went to his car to get a big basket of apples that he had brought from his farm. Grandma followed Mrs. Hansen and her daughter into the dining cottage.

It was as nicely-furnished inside as the schoolrooms. The walls had been painted gray and yellow by the Spooners and there were new brown-topped tables and brown-trimmed chairs. Kitchen utensils hung over the big shiny oil stove and the familiar poster, "Wash your hands," hung over the gray sink.

Miss Hansen showed her parents where to sit. Grandma pushed Mrs. Two Bears aside and seated herself beside Mrs. Hansen. In a huff, the PTA president went to sit beside her husband at another table.

Mr. Hansen seemed to realize that the president was insulted. He turned to his table companions. "I go sit vith the Four Bears," he said in a loud voice, with a twinkle in his blue eyes. His daughter frowned at him as if he were a naughty pupil, but all the Indians laughed. They liked jokes. Mrs. Two Bears laughed good-naturedly too.

Alice passed the hamburgers at Miss Hansen's table. She was so busy looking at Mrs. Hansen that she dropped two of them on the floor. Many of the men and boys had taken their plates outside since there wasn't enough room at the tables. But Frankie ate his food standing behind Grandma's chair. He didn't want to miss anything. Alice passed the salad to Mrs. Hansen and told her that she didn't have to eat any if she didn't want to.

Grandma could hardly "chaw" for looking at Mrs. Hansen.

"You American citizen?" she asked.

"Oh, ya," replied the Norwegian lady enthusiastically. "Ve come from Norvay because ve vanted to be American citizens. Ve studied it and took the examination. Now ve got our papers."

"Me citizen too," boasted Grandma. "Government make me citizen. Big paper in Washington. Why you leave Norvay?"

Grandma supposed that Norvay was some town east of the Missouri River.

"Olaf and me vanted to live in such fine free land for our children," said Mrs. Hansen. "Here everyone has equal chance. Think of it. Ve come here with nothing. Ve vork hard and now ve got fine farm with big red barn and apple orchards. It could not happen in Norvay ven ve vere young."

"Where Norvay?" asked Grandma. "In South Dakota?"

"Oh, no," replied Mrs. Hansen. "It's vay across the ocean."

"You educated?" asked Grandma Tomahawk.

"No," said Mrs. Hansen regretfully. "Ve didn't get that chance because ve grew up in old country."

"Old-time Indian school no good too," said Grandma. "Learn English and wash hands. Government give Indian good school now. White man more civilized nowdays."

"But our Anna's got a good education," put in Mrs. Hansen. "That is vy this is such a vonderful country. Here our Anna graduated from college. And you know vat she said to me the day she graduated? So pretty she vas in her cap and gown and diploma tied vith ribbon. She said, 'Mama, it is a vonderful thing to be a teacher. Perhaps some boy I teach vill be president of the United States.' That's vat our Anna said."

"You mean Indian boy in this school?" asked Grandma in amazement.

"Vy not?" demanded Mrs. Hansen. "In this country it is possible."

Grandma turned in her chair and looked at Frankie. There was an expression in his eyes as if he were seeing an Indian boy's vision. He was seeing where the white man's road could lead him.

"My Frankie president of United States?" asked Grandma in awe.

"Vy not?" demanded Mrs. Hansen again. "Our Anna is good teacher."

Grandma was spechless for the rest of the meal. She ate her cake and drank her coffee with a faraway look in her eyes. Mr. Hansen's apples from the fine farm with the big red barn were passed around and Grandma cut hers into slices so that she could chew it. But she had little to say.

The meal finished, all of the company trooped back to the community cabin for the PTA meeting. Grandma followed in Mrs. Hansen's steps. She sat beside her on a bench.

Then Mrs. Two Bears called the meeting to order. She began to write names on the shaky blackboard while her husband and Mr. Hansen held it steady.

"As you know," she told the audience, "this meeting is to elect officers for the coming year. It should have been held before school was out last year, but the attendance dwindled so." She looked over the names. "We have a slate with Elizabeth Red Eagle and myself for president," she said. "Are there any nominations from the floor?"

There was no comment, then Mrs. Hansen quickly stood up. "I nominate Mrs. Tomahawk," she said. "She is the only grandmother here and she has a great interest in education. Ve have been talking about it during supper."

Everyone was as surprised as if Jim Sees Hawk had been nominated for president. They stared at each other. There was a buzz of voices while Mrs. Two Bears disdainfully wrote "Esther Tomahawk" on the blackboard.

The buzzing voices disagreed at first then began to murmur more softly. Yes, Mrs. Hansen's mother was right. Grandma Tomahawk had the wisdom of age. Once the Indians had greatly respected age. They still did. Why hadn't someone thought of Grandma Tomahawk before?

So votes were cast and Esther Tomahawk was elected the new president of the PTA. "And now we're going to discuss plans for getting the school buildings painted and the doors repaired before winter," said Mrs. Two Bears because she was in no hurry to give up her authority.

The men began shuffling restlessly. One of them rose to go out for a smoke. A couple of others started to follow. PTA was really women's business, remarked one of them.

But Grandma Tomahawk rose imperiously.

"You men sit down," she commanded. "PTA everybody's business."

Then realizing the great dignity of the speech which she was about to make, she used the Sioux language. She spoke eloquently with many gestures, like the true daughter of a chief. She spoke the way she would have spoken if she had been elected to the tribal council.

Alice, her duties in the dining cottage ended, sat on the floor with her eyes on Grandma. She was so proud of her. Grandma was like teacher's parents. She wore the clothing of her people and spoke broken English but she was a real American citizen. She could lead people when the need arose.

Frankie had slipped away from the dishwashing when the word was relayed to him that his

grandmother was the new president of the PTA. He was peeping through the doorway.

Suddenly Grandma Tomahawk realized that some of her listeners could not understand the Indian language. She grinned at them mischievously. "Me say everybody fix school," she explained. "Not fit for president of United States with broken doors and no paint. Saturday everybody meet and paint. Big chaw after."

The meeting finally broke up and the Tomahawks headed home in the White Eagle car. Frankie still didn't know what would happen about the potato picking in Nebraska. He finally mustered up courage to ask.

"Do we have to go to Nebraska with the Iron Shells, Grandma?" he asked.

The old woman snorted. "Potato picking. Me make big joke. Course you stay in school. Peoples come all way from Norvay across the ocean to go our school."

Frankie was satisfied.

Grandma was quiet for a long time then she began chuckling to herself. "Me Great White Father of PTA," she giggled.

They were home at last. They thanked the White Eagles and shook hands all around. Grandma reminded them that they were to help at the school on Saturday regardless of what program was on their new TV.

Alice hurried into the cabin and lighted the kerosene lamp. The flame lit Grandma's face as she stood in the doorway. Her hawk eyes looked all around, pouncing on one defect after another.

"This house need fixing too," she declared. "Need whitewash and new curtains. Not fit for president of PTA."

She and Alice went to sleep in the bed. Frankie curled up on a pallet on the floor. Tomorrow he would confess to Miss Hansen about how he had tricked Grandma into going to the PTA supper. Teacher would understand.

He could hear the wind rising outside. He heard a coyote howl far off on the prairie. But it was cozy and comfortable inside the cabin. Its logs clasped the Tomahawks like fingers, holding them tightly together.

2432

4060